Too Good To Be Used

A NOVEL

by

R. Lee Walker

Printed

2007

TRAFFORD
PUBLISHING™

• Canada • UK • Ireland • USA •

ISBN: 978-1-4120-3159-2 (sc)
ISBN: 978-1-4269-4530-4 (hc)

Trafford rev. 12/01/2011

 www.trafford.com

North America & international
toll-free: 1 888 232 4444 (USA & Canada)
phone: 250 383 6864 ♦ fax: 812 355 4082

ACKNOWLEDGEMENTS

There are a number of wonderful people who contributed in countless ways to my experiences in writing this book.

My gratitude to my family who generously shared their time to read my manuscript. Special thanks goes to my early reviewers Fesia Davenprort, Sheila Funderburk, Dr. Cathleen Lovette, Maxine Thompson, Lee White, and a special thanks to Laverne Walker for her encouragment. Also, thank you to my editor Candi Cross.

Most of all, I give God the glory for giving me the energy to get the work done.

CHAPTER *One*

FALL 2001

Della's fingers dripped green. Not green with emotion, but green from the still life watercolor painting she was working on. A tree was not the most glamorous object to paint, but she was determined to stroke the canvas until the paint blob was unmistakably a tree. The late night exercise not only served as a new hobby for Della but a creative distraction from caseloads, real estate moguls, and commercial finance statements—the ones that were usually exaggerated anyway. When all you had to go on was fifty pages of numerals handed over by a crooked accountant, picking out the real figures from the false was like trying to climb Mount Everest without gear. If she could excel in this process day after day, she could surely paint a darned tree, Della thought.

She sipped from a glass of chardonnay and examined the watercolor. It was actually starting to look like a brown monster with green hair. "Art shall not be forced in this room," said Mrs. Pope the night before as a student angrily flipped over his palette on the floor. Apparently he couldn't mix the proper blend of red to paint the model's lips. "Well, art ain't gonna be forced in this room neither, child," Della said to herself.

Della had reluctantly taken her therapist's suggestion to set up the art station in her home. The goal was to prove that she could accomplish something outside the world of law. Dr. Venus had pegged her as an "uncooperative, self-righteous baby" the first hour she had counseled Della, so following an instruction now and then had to be worth the astronomical bill. *In love and hate, attorneys and doctors belonged together*, was the poor people's mantra. Della would have rather spent the fees at Aron's art supply each week but a promise was a promise to her best friend Neilmore. The one who insisted she would be by her side forever. Talking to someone neutral about her narcissism and penchant for sadistic men would iron it all out eventually, Neilmore swore.

Della's eyes burned through the stack of papers on her desk just a few feet away. They begged for attention like a dangerously high fever. For two weeks, she had been negotiating with a private equity lender tirelessly for a client in Honolulu who had grand dreams but no money to make them happen. Instead of saving money for the hotel property, Della guessed that Mr. Kupchak had snorted the funds away. His eyes were wide and his mouth flailed every time they discussed business. Considering she had dated a couple of cokeheads, Della could certainly spot one when she saw him.

No matter if their meetings were five hours or ten, Kupchak refused to sit down. This made Della guzzle several cups of coffee just to keep up. She resented the unhealthy pattern that someone else had fueled in her—even on time she was getting paid handsomely for. Health-conscious since the high school days of track and field, Della became a fitness fanatic the hour she turned thirty. "After your twenties, you'll lose that body if you don't schmooze that body," her mother once said. From then on, she spent a fortune on protein shakes, oxygenated water, mineral facials, and kickboxing sessions.

Della wanted to close the case desperately. She was fed up with Wanda Durham's endless questions. Known as a sly fox at the firm, Wanda's competitive meddling was incessant. How many digits are attached to the property? Have you drafted a brokerage agreement yet? Are you sure you're doing everything for your client? Why doesn't Kupchak meet with you in Atlanta? Do you know how much time you're costing the firm by jumping on that plane again?

No matter how hard Della worked, blondie Wanda followed inches behind, holding a gigantic match over Della's confidence. Sometimes she felt like they were more like rival sistas than coworkers, and Wanda's support was offered as a chance to spy. Had Wanda not insisted she was in a relationship, Della supposed they would have competed for the same men too. Another partner at the firm even labeled them sisters—"tall, top of the line living dolls" he called them—while Della seethed. She resented being compared to any woman, let alone someone who, she perceived, was out to wreck her career.

Winning the "Hawaii hot spot" case would also allow Della to splurge on another vacation. A trip to Aruba cooed in the horizon, but she hadn't been able to get away for three months. She was used to going somewhere every other month. Besides practicing law, traveling (and not cheap road trips) was her greatest passion. She took pride in having visited thirty countries. From the deserts in Ghana to the pyramids in Egypt, Della had taken in much of the world through seeing places that most people only read about. And for all the sights she took in, there was usually a hot romance to go with them.

There was Tamari who kissed her under the eucalyptus tree in Zimbabwe.

Jean Paul danced with her for seven hours at a discothèque in Paris before they talked for more hours on the train. Figaro played the saxophone for Della in his wine cellar in Florence.

Della knew all these impulsive escapades were dangerous, but they invigorated her like no other guilty pleasure. Fearing scorn, she had only shared the details of *half* her sessions with Neilmore, who was rather conventional when it came to romance.

While Neilmore had a sassy look with all those hot curls piled high on her head and spaghetti strap heels to match every low-cut club outfit, Della guessed her to be an absolute prude in bed. Considering Neilmore's lectures about "high risk sex," Della wondered if she should be an abstinence counselor instead of an attorney.

Della took her glass of tea to the kitchen in search of a morning snack. She decided to finish the watercolor that evening at 6PM. She figured that slowly munching on something would relax her mind. Della had always admired the hours her sister Jamie poured into drawing mock-up blueprints for an architecture class. The only reason Jamie would stop was for another glass of sweet tea and butter cookie.

Jamie taught Della that all creative people were large consumers. Cigarettes. Bourbon. Food. Coffee. Sex. Coupled with excessive appetites, creative types were also ten times more likely to be depressed or suicidal. Great, Della thought, that takes care of 80 percent of the men I date!

Suddenly there was a thunderous knock on Della's door. She set the glass of wine down. Her heart thumped wildly. Della glanced at the clock—12:05, five minutes since she had last checked. She had no idea who it could be. The sound of fist hitting wood bounced under her bare feet. "Miss James, it's the police, we know you're in there, open the door!" The voice was threatening. Della wondered if he intended to break the door in. She sprang to action.

"Just a minute!" she exclaimed while adjusting her robe. Taking in her father's constant chatter about crooked cops, Della disliked the police.

Della unlocked the door, opening it just enough to catch sight of the other side. "What do you want? I did not call you," she said. "Perhaps you're looking for my neighbors?" It was worth a shot. The Latin couple in the house next door fought every other night.

"If you're Miss James, we're looking for you. You're talking to APD, now let us in!"

Della fearfully stepped back. She had a gut-wrenching feeling that peanut butter parfaits, chardonnay and watercolor painting were finished for the night.

"Ms. James, I'm Detective Johnson and this is my partner, Detective Williams." Both inspected Della's spacious living room from where they stood. "Let's get to the point: how did you get the white Lexus parked outside?"

Her pink silk robe was tightly tied around her body, but Della pulled the strap again. She resented even the first few moments of this interruption—the boisterous knocking, the macho-cop stance, and the probing eyes. They were surveying her elegant living room like newlyweds buying their first home. "It was given to me as a gift from my boyfriend," Della answered haughtily.

"Fine, where did he get it?" Johnson asked flatly.

"He bought it from a car lot downtown, and I was there."

"You were there?" Johnson was clearly the dominant one of the pair. Williams seemed more enchanted by her collection of Oriental antiques than the matter at hand. Placed around the room with accent lighting, the decorative figurines and teapots were a showstopper for many upon entrance. "I asked you a question, Ms. James." Johnson wasn't only authoritative, he was an impatient little asshole, Della thought.

"As I said, yes, I was there when he bought it."

"Ms. James, you need to come with us."

"I don't need to do anything," Della replied. She hadn't the foggiest idea what they would want with her and she was well-read on her rights. They didn't appear to have an arrest warrant. "Are you familiar with the Goldberg Law Firm, officers?"

Neither answered her question. Johnson stepped closer to Della and grabbed her elbow lightly. "That vehicle is stolen and we have an arrest warrant, Ms. James. You are a suspect. You have the right to remain silent. You have the right to an attorney. If you can't afford one, one will be provided for you. Do you understand the Miranda Rights I've just given you?"

Della was too surprise to reply. Could confusion cause a heart attack? The possibility seemed very real to Della. "I told you we drove it out of the car lot together. You must be referring to another Lexus, now please let go of me!"

"We'll take you out kicking and holding your feet, Ms. James. Put on your clothes and come with us." Della wondered if the other detective even had a voice. Williams looked as scared as she was.

"I'm an attorney of good character. I will meet you at the station in an hour. I know exactly where it is." Della realized she was expressing words of desperation that carried no weight at this point. She was a trapped animal cowering in front of the semi's headlights.

"That's not an option. You must come with us now." Johnson grabbed her arm while Williams stepped aside.

"Get your hands off me. I'm not a hood rat!" Della reacted with a physical fury as her father always urged her to do once "an undesirable" touched her. She wished he were there. "I don't have a criminal record. Can we talk about all this here?"

"Ms. James, you have the right to remain silent. Anything you say can be held against you in a court of law." Della struggled from Johnson's grasp. The passive Williams finally stepped up from behind and pulled her arms back with force.

"Do not resist!" Williams shouted.

Della bowed her head as she sunk deeper into the backseat of the police cruiser. Maybe if she concentrated real hard, she thought senselessly, she would be back in the study painting the tree. *How could this happen? I'm too smart to be used like this!* Della never dreamed that she would be handcuffed for anything… even sex. She was downright claustrophobic. That's why the closet was never an option during a game of her sister Jamie's version of "lost and found" when they were children.

As the cruiser left Della's street, she started to cry. She smelled her own sweat and wanted to scream. Outside of a few bad character assessments of men, Della felt like she had always exercised good judgment in her decision-making. Both shining examples of successful, upstanding citizens, Della's parents had taught her to believe in herself and be independent. Of course, a stylish car would not be worth compromising that integrity—she could have afforded her own if it were that important.

She could not fathom what Edward Dawson had possibly done. No, Della had not driven the car off the lot as she had told the officers. But she had been on Edward's arm when he asked her to pick out a car that "dazzled her brown eyes and made her heart sing." What meaningless words to remember at a time like this, Della thought. Edward was always coming up with romantic catchphrases.

"Give us what we want and you'll be back in that palace of yours before you know it, Ms. James," Johnson barked from the driver's seat. Della was getting sick of hearing her name come out of the pigheaded detective's mouth. Della surveyed her meager surroundings. Fingerprints on the window, cigarette burns on the seat, blood on the carpet. She was utterly nauseous.

"Apparently, I don't have what you want because I have no idea why I'm sitting in this filthy car of yours!" There was a small measure of satisfaction in being sarcastic no matter that Dr. Venus said Della's mouth was like a rusty blade.

"All in good time, Ms. James, all in good time. Make yourself comfortable. Would you like the air conditioner on?"

Della refused to answer. Each bump in the road made her feel worse. She wondered how long it would be until she could make a phone call. Of course Neilmore would be absolutely dumbfounded. Her dramatic Aquarius friend was always receptive to a good story, but this would be unheard of.

That said, Della couldn't wait to hear the treacherous details herself. The drive seemed like an endless journey to the twilight zone, aimless and frightening. Paranoia crept through Della's system. It seemed like everyone in the streets of Atlanta and in the cars alongside the cruiser was trying to see her. *That's right, gawk; this is your city's finest - trying to pin a stolen car on an educated, hardworking, Black lawyer.* Della almost shouted the inner chatter. Her arms were going numb from the tightness of the handcuffs.

"Detectives, I don't think I can make it much longer before vomiting all over this hideous seat," Della said. "Can you stop the car?"

"I think she's getting carsick, Johnson," said Williams. "Pull over. She's harmless." said Williams. Johnson pulled the car to the side of Peachtree Street. He helped Della out of the backseat and loosened her handcuffs. The men turned away as Della gagged and vomited for five minutes. Both helped her back into the car, relieved that she didn't put up a fight. Club goers and prostitutes walked past and made comments to one another. One was brave enough to blow a stream of smoke into Johnson's face.

"Watch it, dirty little punk. You better hope I don't see you again when I'm off duty," said Johnson. His particularly calm voice was almost chilling. The pink-haired raver just snickered in a drug haze and continued on with his three look-alike friends.

After shutting her eyes for a few minutes, Della saw the police department directly ahead. In no time, she was escorted to the interrogation office and expected to answer what seemed like a million questions about Edward Dawson. He was the suave pilot she had met at the Hartsfield Airport months ago. Johnson asked her if she was involved with him at the present time. She didn't know how to answer the question.

When Della could get away from David, her pseudo-boyfriend, she would meet Edward in various locations. His friend's mansion on the plush side of Buckhead, a hotel downtown or a resort in another city—it was always an adventure upon his suggestion.

"I see him from time to time," Della said flatly. She looked down at herself in the girly pink robe and cringed. Now Della wished that she would have been rational enough to change into a power suit. In fact, the Donna Karan black one would have instantly instilled some confidence in her.

"You must tell us where to find him right away, Ms. James," said Williams.

Della almost exploded into laughter. Edward could not be easily tracked down. In fact, he had always found *her* when they were both ready to see each other again. He told her that he didn't keep a permanent address because of his demanding job as a pilot. There was no permanent phone number either, just a direct pager system strictly for communication with AirWave, his employer. "Ha, Edward could be flying over the Swiss Alps or Costa Rica for all I know. He won't be found by anyone until he wants to be."

"What is that supposed to mean? You should be

aware that Edward Dawson is a very wanted man, Ms. James. Are you willing to take a lie detector test?"

She gladly agreed to take the test, anything to escape the dingy confines. Della passed the test, which affirmed that she did not knowingly accept stolen property. Next, Johnson asked her to point Edward out in a series of photographs. From pages and pages of crooks, there was no match. Just as Della assumed the ordeal was done, the detectives told her that she was being charged with conspiracy.

"What? Why? I demand to know what the hell is going on right now!"

Della's breath was shallow.

"We need you to calm down so you can think logically and explain some things for us," said Williams. Their audacity irritated Della. Honestly, she had not spoken to Edward in months.

She told the police that the last happy hour blast they shared—whiskey sours for him, margaritas for her—Della confessed that she had not shaken off David yet. She wasn't sure she actually wanted to either. That night, Edward literally went into a temper tantrum at the Sun Dial bar and slammed the eight ball glass on the table. Seventy-two floors above the city and their romantic interlude had been cut short by Della's candidness. When she asked Edward if he were sleeping with others (she assumed he was), he became even more incensed. At this point in their excursions, Della had found Edward to be incredibly pushy for a commitment, but he had little time to even give her.

On the other hand, while quite unadventurous in bed and just generally dull, David was intellectually stimulating, successful and financially stable. *And* he had never gotten her into trouble. David also came from a good family—something that Della's parents commended. They didn't demand much from her outside of a solid education, but having both grown up in the Deep South where blood was thicker than water, Della's mother and father preferred her to be paired with a man who had a sense of his roots.

The detectives urged Della to make a phone call while they were feeling "generous." Her kind of generosity would have come in the form of diamonds, or in this case, a ride back home... pronto. The real reason for offering the five minutes, however, was because they assumed the interaction with someone close would calm her down. They were convinced that whether apple pie recipes or lazy husbands, the subject matter between women contained the same urgency.

Della would definitely ring Neilmore, who would surely assume she was calling from some exotic soiree in a yacht or limousine at this hour. "Della, baby, calm down. I can't make out a word you're saying. Lay off the liquor, will ya?" Neilmore's response was mild. Della's words came out in one sloppy gush. She sighed.

"Neilmore, I'm in jail. Do you hear me? Jail! I'm at the precinct downtown for a stolen car and conspiracy. I don't believe this!" Della squealed.

The best friend a girl could have at a time like this, Neilmore did not drill Della with questions. She promised that she would be there in thirty minutes with a change of clothes for Della. Neilmore had no idea that Della had been dragged into the station in her robe, but they both knew how polished she could be. The image of Della sitting in a filthy interrogation room—or much worse—naturally bothered her friend of ten years. It never occurred to Della that Edward could be in Atlanta.

CHAPTER *Two*

You could say Della was born a diva. It was as though life was a throne bearing her signature. She sat on its plush cushion and embraced the many privileges that came with the seat. Power, titles, money, men. More men. It's not that she dismissed all the things Neilmore "preached" at her. She just didn't have time to live in the past or simply care about the past like Neilmore did. Defying the psychoanalytical way of living—looking to the past, learning from the past, reliving traumas and feelings of loss—Della lived her days solidly in the moment. *Let the good times roll.* After college, she felt like she deserved to.

Della had arrived on the law scene with the right credentials at the right time. She had arrived at a time that she and Neilmore called the "Downsize Hallelujah Thank You Telecommute Days." Della could always throw in a few more "amens" than her buddy Neilmore could, since most of Della's work was done from home.

Sure, Della had a good civil litigation caseload from Goldberg Law Firm, but she had steadily been building up her own clientele from her father's connections. Because Della knew her stuff, referrals spread like wild fire. A lot of business folks took pride in working with a skilled female attorney and there was everything right about keeping it in the family, so to speak. Whatever Della could not manage, she'd see if Neilmore wanted the challenge before sending the referral on to some other litigator. Neilmore would do the same.

The strategy was a game plan they dreamed up at Harvard, a game plan that Neilmore forced into action once they were both working attorneys. She was very particular about playing by the rules they devised. Della had once told Neilmore, "Girl, you are way into recycling Black dollars too much for me. Recycling *all* dollars is the game I'd rather play. Do you think the White power structure is going to take away what you've earned? Baby, we need to unify with anyone, green or red, in need of an attorney."

Neilmore replied, "Sleeping beauty, you can wake up now," and reminded Della that fifty-five percent of her caseload came from her family's referrals, Black entrepreneurs in Atlanta and beyond.

Despite their differences, Neilmore would always be grateful to Della for bringing her to Atlanta. After Neilmore's mother died, there was no point in going back to New York City, a dreary place as it was before the loss. And eventually, if Neilmore stayed on the right track, she'd soon have a robust clientele just like Della. She wanted nothing more than to leave her day job, where throats were cut as often as salaries.

It took a while for Della to adjust to the in-house politics at Goldberg. Wanda Durham—the only other female working at the firm—had already spead her influence all over the place. As soon as she got the job years ago, Della had called Neilmore from the lounge next door to the firm with drink already in hand, screaming, "Who's this day about, girl? It's about me! I got the job! Join me at Leopard Lounge and watch me tell everyone that I'm an attorney next door. I'll have your drink ready!"

Thereafter, it was a ritual to report to Neilmore the day's happenings at the firm like the nightly news.

Like sister magic, Neilmore got her first job out of Harvard a week later at Harold and Davidson, another top law firm in Atlanta. Thanks to letters of referral from Della's father and other influential Atlantans, they'd been exchanging office news every day since.

Neilmore would say, "Now you know what's going on in my scandalous firm. Top that! What's the latest at Goldbug Booger and what's Wanda, the Goldbug Booger Digger doing today to make your life miserable?"

Everyone at Goldberg knew that Wanda was taken by a mysterious someone but pretended to be smitten by Jeremy Goldberg, the lead partner. It was a tiring episode; Wanda pushing her sex appeal on the main man, even though she was not genuinely attracted to him. He was happily married anyway, so it seemed. The games that intelligent, successful women played were the same that stupid, trifling ones played. When Wanda thought she was being smart getting Jeremy to kick Della off intake counsel status and place her in telecommute status half of the year, Della was delighted.

Della told Neilmore that Wanda couldn't stand her heat around Jeremy in the office. "Neilmore, you know there is no limit to what the Digger won't do to keep the scent of a real woman away from the main dog's muzzle."

In truth, Della never desired going out with the boys to get ahead. She knew that sleeping around with coworkers bred messy consequences. While magnetically beautiful, she could subtly flaunt the goods without wreaking havoc with them. There was just a delicate balance to achieve. Della recognized early on that she could prepare a case better than anybody and argue the case as if her life depended on winning. That said, every company had a vision of its players and fitting the model of who they wanted would necessitate certain attitude adjustments. If she took a real personality test, Della would be falling off the chart in the areas of confidence, competitiveness, and self-indulgence.

"Once the big dogs get past your high hips and funny little pout," her daddy had said, "talent will be your most valuable asset and you better be prepared to shake a finger and teach those boys who the new boss is."

Della knew it. And with that knowledge, she would persevere.

CHAPTER *Three*

Proof is the last thing you need when you love living your life as a lie. Looking through the criminal files in Marlon's office, Della found it difficult to focus. Necessary, but unbearably difficult.

Blinded by all she claimed to be because she could and would pay any price to buy whatever satisfied her, Della moved through the police files, slowly hoping not to find her lover's face.

"Della James!" Marlon Richards gleefully welcomed his sister-in-law. He took her wrap and pulling out the only chair that was freed of folders and paperwork, insisted that she sit. "Sister-in-law, it ain't everyday one of Atlanta's top nine Black women barristers comes to visit a lowly public servant. Make yourself at home."

Della sat down and studied Marlon closely. "You

act as if you're uncomfortable being the highest paid district attorney in Atlanta. Why, Marlon?"

"Why am I the Fulton County District Attorney, why ain't I comfortable or why do I fall back on easy conversation in the company of friends?"

"Friends? That's rich, even for you, Marlon. Do you use *friends* meaning your wife is letting you and me be *friends* today and it's okay because she says so? Or are you retreating to poetry and metaphor, implying we should make *friendly* conversation even when we probably have nothing *friendly* to say to each other at all?"

"Della, Della, it's been twelve years. And well…"

There was nothing Marlon could say to Della to soothe her ruffled ego.

There was a time when Della controlled Marlon and losing that control bothered her. Even if he was married to her sister now and had been with Jamie for twelve years, Della's vanity made Marlon her catch, not Jamie's. Too bad he was the marrying kind when she was not. Too bad Jamie wanted him when she did not. She didn't mind them being together as much as she minded Jamie commanding the game and shutting her out of their lives for years.

Marlon had been crazy about Della, and everyone who knew them, including Della's sister, knew it. Marlon belonged to Della then. They had been freshmen political science majors together at the time. Della had seen through Marlon's country boy willingness to become cosmopolitan.

It was funny how Della could do for others what she could not do for herself —make them feel whole and validated.

She took away Marlon's insecurities about coming to Atlanta to college. Atlanta challenged Marlon. It was the first time in his life he was away from Midville, Georgia, a two-mile city with a population of about five hundred. Della changed the myth of his insecurities.She made him at home in the city within a city called "Della." Privately, she screwed him senseless and made him repeat her name as his one and only address. Publicly, she let him bask in her golden boldness and all-knowing city smarts. When he had all that down pat and was ready to surprise Della with something of his own knowing, ready to propose marriage to her, she clipped his wings, cut him off and flew away.

Marlon loved Della still because she made him feel at home in the big city. She introduced him to her family. When his family came to Atlanta, they were welcomed guests at the James' home. Marlon stayed in Atlanta for grad school at Georgia Tech, then wildly ended up at Emory Law School while Della, bored with everything familiar, dumped Marlon and Atlanta and set out to study law at Harvard.

"Well," Marlon continued, "forgive me, Della. I mean, forgive my colloquialisms. It's rare around here to be able to enjoy good, down home talk. Hell, I don't need to tell you about the plight of qualified African American attorneys in public and private positions, do I?"

"No. No, you don't, Marlon, and since we're doing colloquialisms, too bad. Too bad you're the first Black district attorney Atlanta has ever seen I believe. Too bad if it's hoodrat conversation with all two of your homies back in Midville (population, 457) you're missing. I'm not here for all that. I'm not here to discuss old times or your homies or hard times on the corporate plantation for unemployed, qualified African American attorneys. If that's what you called me here to talk about, I'm leaving. I've got work to do." Della reached for her wrap and purse.

Damn, Marlon thought, what a ball buster she still is. How am I going to tell her the deep mess she's in?

"None of the above?" Della felt like pressing on for the hell of it. "Then, no doubt you pulled me from my busy caseload to tell me just how you and my sister's divine marriage is going? What? Is there another anniversary coming up I need to miss?

Your ninth? Should I even bother to send a gift this year?"

"I wish, Della. I wish things were that simple today. First, let's make peace. And then be prepared to listen very carefully. I would not have called you down here for petty family grudges, and at this point, that's exactly what you're squeezing between those melons of yours—a family grudge." Marlon was obviously through with playing the nice guy. He held out his hand to shake Della's.

"Guessing game is over, Marlon. What am I doing here? Are you trying to con me?" She lightly smacked his palm in halfhearted acceptance of the peace gesture.

"Maybe you're not as sharp as you used to be with country bumpkins. Maybe you're confusing me with *Edward*. Have a look at these."

Hearing her lover's name—the one who had supposedly stolen a beautiful Lexus for her, which forced the police to take it from her, which forced her to drive around in a mediocre rented car—pulled Della to the edge of her seat. She had not heard from him since being arrested and she wasn't sure she would ever hear from him again.

While Della suffered through turning pages and trying to focus on the shocking content, Marlon was not happy. Rather than exit the room for the donuts on the secretary's desk he'd been craving, he stayed with her. He was not turned on by watching her deteriorate. He wanted to be there to offer support, even if she rejected it.

Della James, Marlon remembered the freshman bombshell who liberated him from the sticks in the '80s. *Della, still petite with a whisper of luscious softness to a rough and buffed farm boy. Her light skin still looks so buttery.* Marlon knew it wasn't a great time for such thoughts, including his improvisational poetry, but he seriously wanted to get over the past. Knowing what the Feds discovered about Edward, Marlon intuitively knew that Della's hardened interior would shatter.

He read Della's face and watched disappointment sap her the moment she identified Edward's photo, the moment she comprehended the long string of Edward's aliases. When Della's face saddened, Marlon searched for words of comfort. Poetry in motion would not do. Marlon wanted to give Della back some of what she first gave him: strength on unfamiliar ground.

Marlon interrupted Della's mechanical process of sifting through the papers. He cleared his throat. Della shamefully raised her head from the photos and confidential documents. "'Edward' is only one name he uses. Confident man, huh?" Marlon presented yet another stack of files.

"Yep, con man for sure."

"Guess he got me," Della said. She looked as if she would break down in tears, but Marlon did not expect her to really cry.

Della recovered frighteningly and laughed. "Guess he got me good!

Marlon, how did you know?"

"Look, this chump Edward's a career criminal. The Feds are after him for impersonating a commercial pilot and you're going to be the scapegoat for his sorry butt. Della, your name is on a dozen reference lists for credit cards issued to his aliases, bank statements, the lease to the stolen Lexus, God knows what else. Under the Patriot Act, you've been supporting a criminal, and that makes you a criminal."

Della had to call Marlon's name twice to slow down his stream of rapid talking. She had no idea why she had to take responsibility for someone else's evildoing. Impersonating a commercial pilot was a severe crime. Impersonating a commercial pilot after the country's national security had been blown to pieces on September 11th was a severe, unthinkable crime. Della wondered where she fell into the equation.

"I know all this is very confusing, Della, so let

me explain it very clearly." Marlon sprang to his feet and paced around the room while explaining the Patriot Act.

In line with the president's vehement "war against terrorism," the Act was passed swiftly to provide an all-inclusive combat against anyone thought of as remotely involved. Federal agents were now permitted to use roving wiretaps to track terrorists, conduct impromptu investigations of anyone associated with criminals, and obtain records from stores, libraries, and even doctors' offices to track suspects.

Della was more confused than ever. Authorized roving wiretaps, judicially-approved secret search warrants, access to her business and financial records…. She wanted to call her travel agent for a one-way ticket to Aruba.

"Marlon, I work for a top law firm, I am highly respected in Atlanta, and I've never committed a crime in my entire life. How could I possibly be under investigation for toying with the nation's security?"

"Look, Della, as much as you love to sling around your upstanding title, it doesn't change your circumstances," Marlon said. His voice softened and he sat back down. "You just trusted the wrong guy."

Della dropped her head again weakly. Marlon told her the story of Dr. John Acka Blay-Meizah, who billed himself as the richest man in the world. No one had a larger education or bank account. He was the sole beneficiary of the Oman Ghana fund, a $27 billion dollar trust. The problem was that he needed other people's money to free up the fund. Blay-Mei-zah promised them $10 for every dollar they gave him. By the time an investigative reporter discovered him, he was living in luxury in London, due to the gullibility and greed of his American investors whom he'd funneled more than $200 million from.

Besides hearing about the greatest con man that ever was, Della had to sit through a brief documentary on "professional tricksters." She cringed at the title, "Escaping the Tricksters." Marlon had no interest in making her see the stupid film, but it was required by the Feds. The cheesy voiceover blared over the speaker unit while Della stared at the screen, blank-faced.

"Tricksters have the appearance of goodness that enables them to take advantage of others, taking all they can get, legally or illegally. These folks live through their possessions, and material wealth means a great deal to them, although they may affect a humble attitude. It is not the mugger in the alley or obvious shady characters we need to fear, for we have learned their ways. Disguised with charming manners and a pleasant demeanor, real danger lurks in an overly attentive new acquaintance that offers friendship easily and sporadically withdraws it. These tricksters are afraid to get close to anyone they can't completely control, for fear their cheating ways will be unmasked. It may seem they are offering companionship, but this is only a mirage, acted out to gain your confidence. Does confidence and conmen ring a bell?"

Della blocked her ears with her hands. She'd had enough of the elementary infomercial on how to spot tricksters. Marlon turned off the film.

"So, Della, con men come in all appearances. They lure people of all ages into money-making schemes and partnerships to separate them from their money, and they are very adept at discarding folks who are no longer useful to them or who have already been sucked dry. They are cold, calculating bloodsuckers that act out of mindless ambitions with no heart to speak of. You're one of a long list of professional Black women that this loser has swindled money from."

Marlon had gotten really incensed. Della just wanted to go home and hibernate. Of course, now she knew that any minute the Feds could wire her house, office or car, and she would have no real privacy to speak of.

CHAPTER *Four*

As disappointing as it was to finally see Edward Dawson's face in a book of police photos, Della couldn't help admitting to herself how fine he looked even in a mug shot. "I must be absolutely sick," Della said to herself after leaving the station in a daze.

The day they met, Edward had dazzled Della.

After deboarding at Hartsfield-Jackson Atlanta International, she, like everyone else on his or her way to Atlanta, was moving fast to get out of the packed airport. Within minutes, she was unexpectedly shoved onto the escalator.

All Della remembered was a pair of firm hands grabbing her by the waist to keep her from falling forward and how when she turned around, there his face was. Those green eyes. Those flawless teeth. That boyish smile. That steal-a-touch butter squash skin. The hat. The uniform. The brass bars. Those shining shoes.

. "Are you all right?" the pilot had asked. Della had returned his sure smile and nodded, Yes, I'm all right, even though she could not speak. With the heat of the pilot's hands still on her waist, she did her best to turn around and get off the escalator more efficiently than she had gotten on.

His hands, she would never forget his manly hands. The veins. The definition of his sturdy fingers. They reminded Della of her father's hands. How many days had she stood by him just to watch his hands as he refinished "Mama's junk" exactly the way she instructed for one of her antique shops?

Carrying nothing but her roll-on bag, she exited Hartsfield-Jackson and became embraced by Atlanta's brisk November twilight. And there he was again.

"Miss?"

Della turned in the direction of his voice but said nothing. Nice hands and all, she wasn't into being "chosen." She preferred commanding the selection process: Zoning in on the desirable target, moving in calmly, and then taking it by force, whether by revealing a little skin or exchanging charming banter. Della smiled a little and turned away. With those hands, Edward folded both of hers in his and slipped in a business card. Della was not displeased. She was a little rattled but not displeased.

"My name's Edward Dawson. You're an absolutely stunning woman and I would be honored to bring a dose of happiness into your life. Give me a call. Tomorrow perhaps? We'll go for coffee, okay? I would be delighted to listen to all your stories. Please?" The man was certainly not at a loss for flattering words, Della thought. They were a little too honey-coated for her taste, but she was not turned off by any means.

As she walked in the direction of where she parked her car, Della had deliberately unbuttoned her coat and let the wind cool her. She smiled and tucked Edward's card in her bag. My sweet Jesus, she thought, what strong hands. With this sight implanted in her head, Della had called the next day for coffee. It wasn't until the present, sitting in Marlon's office months later, that Della realized how downhill everything tumbled after that cup of coffee.

CHAPTER *Five*

Arriving for Della only an hour after they spoke to meet for coffee, Edward had opened the passenger door to the rental car, a black-on-black Lincoln Town car. He said, "Thank you, beautiful Della for giving me a chance to make you happy."

Once she slid into the seat and inhaled his magnificent cologne, Della recovered from the surprise. She thought they were taking a cab.

Completely trashing her guard, Della found herself revealing more about her life to Edward than she had shared with anyone. In the three hours they first spent together, he had probably collected enough information to write the biography on Della James.

Edward was less generous with the details of his life. He was thirty-five years old, a pilot, and much of his life revolved around flying to exotic places.

Trained at the prestigious London Metropolitan University, he belonged to flying clubs all over the world. Della was immediately drawn to his knowledge of some of the same places she had been to. In fact, she didn't have anyone in her circle to talk to about Chile, Indonesia, and Japan. The list was endless. When she asked about his family or friends, where he made his permanent home, Edward had shifted in his seat and brought the conversation back to her.

"So what else do you like in this world besides airplanes and fine wine?"

"Well, I think I've already put enough out there about my tastes. What's left to talk about?" Della wasn't being flippant. She was just being herself.

"I can tell there are a lot of things you like in this world. A lady such as yourself—I can tell you pamper yourself and rightly so."

"Okay, I like diamonds."

"Most women do. I know you have wonderful taste. Look at the home you live in. That tells me a lot about you."

"I know everything is interpreted as a message of some sort. I work hard for the things I own."

"So tell me what it's like to be an attorney. Do you take care of the bad guys or the good guys? Are you one of those attorneys I should call when my plane crashes and I need compensation?" Edward's questions were laced with humor, but Della wished just one time in her adulthood she could stay clear of talking about work affairs.

All men wanted to hear about the serial murderers she had sent to Death Row or the crooked mafia bosses she had defended. Women never pressed for those details. One would be surprised what bizarre stories could come from land use cases and property purchases by the wealthiest people in the world.

Edward said, "What a coincidence. I heard about a conservation waste management case your firm is dealing with that could affect my mutual funds. Can you tell me how that's going?"

Impressed, Della gave Edward a briefing on the case she'd been working on for the last six months. He listened attentively.

At the time, she was representing a banking client in connection with the development and construction of a gargantuan commercial project in downtown Atlanta called The Metropon. The project involved 680,000 square feet of retail space, 400 residential apartment units and a 100-unit extended stay hotel. The credit package was comprised of four separate loans aggregating $200 million. Della had to juggle the interests of private financiers, public grants and a life insurance company. All her time, including evenings and weekends, had been dedicated to the case.

She could tell that Edward liked to talk money, even if he couldn't understand all the parts related to the case. He asked her to repeat the amount of the loan and where exactly the property was.

"So you see, I don't do criminal law or personal injury cases," she said.

"I heard worker compensation attorneys are not real attorneys anyway because their case is already laid out," Edward replied.

Della chose her words carefully. She understood the amount of work that was required of workers compensation attorneys. "To some extent that is true, but you still have to argue a case because the other party never wants to settle for your amount. There's still a lot of work involved. The fact of the matter is that an injury did take place and it is documented by medical records. So, do you know anything about law?"

It was his turn to pause. He evaded the question and continued. "So you are constantly battling. Don't you ever get tired of fighting?"

Della ordered a chai latte before responding. She wasn't sure why he was pressing on about her job. It wasn't the most exciting piece of their introductory session. "Edward, I worked very hard to get my job and I work very hard to keep my job. Arguing cases is part of the end result, but the greatest reward is serving someone in need of my expertise."

"Well, what if I were to tell you that I'm in need of your expertise?" Edward didn't skip a beat. He leaned in and folded his hands on the table. Della caught every movement. Inspecting him like a mink coat, she wasn't sure if he was serious or if this was a bad attempt to be seductive. Before she could reply, Edward's cell phone rang and he excused himself.

While Edward was outside, Della freshened up in the restroom. Pulse racing from the espresso, she touched up her mocha lips and ran fingers through her long, straight hair. She thought about ringing the firm to check her voicemail but dismissed the idea. It wasn't everyday that a hot hunk of a man whisked her away in a Lincoln Towncar. And all for coffee! She couldn't wait to find out what dinner would entail.

When Della returned to the table, Edward was there displaying a plate of chocolate cake.

"The sure way to a woman's heart is lots of sugar, yes?" cooed Edward. He had a light spark in his eyes since they broke from one another for a few minutes.

"Is that in exchange for my 'expertise'?"

"We'll talk business after you take a big bite out of

this ooey, gooey dessert." Della complied and licked her lips plentifully. Edward panted.

"Okay, there's more of that to go around. Della, tell me about the company you work for." He took his own small helping of the cake.

"The corporation I work for is just like any other. You have to watch yourself and perform. The others play mind games. If there is a joke that everyone else is laughing at, you must laugh, too. But they won't tell you who the joke is on. Besides the caddy bullshit, the firm has built a reputation worth millions of dollars in wins, and I can be proud of that. Okay, next subject, do you have any brothers and sisters?" When Della was through with something, she was really through.

"I'm more interested in you and everything you have to say," said Edward. "I have always searched for someone like you."

The message was too hokey for Della. "Someone like me? There are scores of pretty, professional women out there. You have no idea who I am."

"That's a valid point, but I felt you right away, Della."

"Felt me? Edward, come on. How many other women have you felt?"

Edward was lost for words at the moment. He looked down at the table and then up at Della with a huge grin. "I know more about you than you think. Your appearance and your confidence tell me a lot."

"Edward, you seem like an intelligent man. Are you always quick to make people judgments?"

"No, absolutely not. I do not judge people." Edward swiped another bite of cake.

Della felt that their conversation had suddenly become inappropriate, considering they had only met.

"Having traveled the world since I was fourteen, I think I'm a good judge of character and can spot a certain type of person."

"Well, what type of person do I appear to be? I could be a maniac. There are many freaks beneath the executive uniforms. You can't tell what's under the dress." The espresso from the cappuccino and ginseng from the chai latte were really kicking into Della's bloodstream now. Edward studied Della, but didn't answer quickly enough.

"Do you think I drive fast, Edward? Do I put the rubber to the medal and speed down the highway recklessly? I have seen some of the nicest people become monsters behind the wheel of a car. They become speed demons literally. My mother was so sweet until she got behind the wheel. I used to ask her, 'Mama, why do you drive so fast?' She would say that she didn't have time to mess around. She just had to get where she was going. My father, on the other hand, was the slowest driver I have ever been in the car with. He would drive down the street in the slow lane unapologetically." Della paused to see if Edward was still in the conversation. He seemed transfixed by her.

"I can see myself in the backseat as a little girl, watching the other cars zoom by. I wanted our car to keep up with them. My mother and I got so annoyed by this. I asked him why he drove so slowly because I thought we were going to be late. Every car passed us. Do you know what he said? I'm not going to a fire and what I want will be there when I get there. Life is going by too fast anyway. Naturally, I did not agree with him."

Edward wasn't sure how to respond. "Della, I'm not a fast driver either. I like to take my time."

"I already guessed that. From the way you talk, you take your time about everything. I need an automatic so I can just get in the car and go. So, does this also mean you are one those brothers who makes love slow too?"

Edward's eyes widened. "I never mentioned anything about sex! If I had, that would have sent off an alarm in your mind and I would probably never see you again. Since you're the woman, you think you can introduce the subject into the conversation and

I'm hooked? How about we not talk about sex right now? We have plenty of time."

"Oh, you want to change the subject because I'm a woman? I bet you talk about sex around the boys."

"What boys?"

"Hmm, don't you have male friends?"

"I don't hang in a clique. If I'm not the leader, I've got to go when someone else tells me to jump. That's not me. You know how cliques try to control you. It's the same protocol as office cliques. They will have you laughing at all the jokes when all the jokes are about you.

Della, you are a quality person, and I know you don't waste time. People on my arm want something out of life. I believe in achieving things together," Edward said sincerely.

"Well, this has certainly been an enlightening conversation."

They mutually agreed to leave the Tarrazu Café. Edward turned on Sade and picked up the conversation. Della, on the other hand, felt like she had revealed enough about herself to last a lifetime.

"I know there was something about me that you liked."

"You think so?" Della replied nonchalantly. If there wasn't something, I wouldn't be in this car with a complete stranger, you cute fool, she thought.

"I do see something, but I'm not going to tell you what it is."

"My job as a pilot tells you a lot. There are things that I know without having obtained a high-priced degree. I don't buy into the 'fool's paradise' if I want to get ahead in life and stay ahead."

"What's the fool's paradise?"

"You know, people who don't have any discipline in their lives. Especially men, who think they can drink all they want, smoke all they want, eat all the junk they want and rampage through the streets all night long. Not to mention drugs! You can't just do a lot of anything and expect to survive and thrive. The word is *moderation*."

"Sounds like you got your head on straight to me. How come you are not married? You are definitely old enough and I know you've been around. What is your story?"

"Must I have a story for you about love and sex?"

"Yes. Everyone has a story why romance didn't work at one time."

"Della, we have a lot of time to talk… at least I certainly hope we do. Must I tell you all my business now? What are you going to do with it? You are just going to pass judgment, walk away and rationalize why I was not the man for you."

Della automatically rolled the window down to cool the heavy dialogue. Edward "I'm not going to judge you. I know we have been doing some deep talking and we just met each other. If you want the truth, I'm in a relationship that I'm getting bored with.

It's not working for me anymore. Sweetheart, I can't afford to waste my precious time anymore."

It was true. David was too busy to entertain Della unless there was a sport or beer involved. And because he was the mayor's accountant, he was constantly immersed in work. David had no sense of adventure.

Edward just stared at Della with nothing to say.

"Edward, does that make you speechless? Plenty of women are in relationships they're tired of and they seek other encounters. That doesn't make us criminals. But hear me out. I'm not desperate for a man no matter how nice he looks."

"Do I look nice to you?"

"Yes, you look nice, all right."

With the quick reply, Edward flashed a charming smile. Della stared straight ahead. "Della, I can tell you make it hard for the average man. He needs a certain amount of education and worldliness to keep up with your appetite. And I know you're the type to investigate the man's family because when you marry the man, you get hitched to the family."

Della contemplated the words *investigate* and *family*. She thought them to be incredibly odd, considering she didn't even know where this man was from. "Don't you think it's a little leading to talk about marriage with a woman you've only known for a couple of hours?"

He again avoided her question. When he accompanied her to the door of her house, Edward asked, "Della, when's the last time anybody treated you special?"

She replied, "It has been a while."

He left her standing in the doorway.

CHAPTER *Six*

Della kept the coffee date with Edward to herself. Neilmore was still trying to persuade her to stay with David, who could potentially settle her down for good. She was not ready to accept that kind of commitment with someone who had never traveled out of the South. He didn't like exotic food. He only made love in the evening with the lights off. And he only listened to rap music, which Della couldn't stand.

Edward had not called for two weeks.

It was a Wednesday and Della had just gotten out of a daunting, six-hour meeting with the movers and shakers involved in the Metropon project. The financiers demanded that the firm call the Metropon the "city of glass" in all press correspondence. Since Della was the point attorney, she caught all the heat when reporters didn't take her instructions. It was a ridiculous, miniscule detail in the larger picture, but there was no way around meeting for hours about such nonsense. *Everything* was relative to the case. The last thing she wanted to do was talk on the phone, but something urged Della to pick up.

"Hey, beautiful. How about you and I getting together for dinner this evening?" Edward asked without identifying himself.

"Gee, I don't know," Della said, already removing her clothes, "I've had a stressful day."

"I'll bring dinner to you. No, it won't be a pizza party with beer."

"You want me to open my house to you like that without notice? You must not know who you're talking to." Edward replied that he wouldn't keep her on the phone and to have a great night.

The production company arrived the next evening. It was a good thing that the cleaning service had just left and Della was settling in with a Woody Allen film. The buzzer rang and she peered outside for a familiar car. There were only a few catering trucks in her peripheral.

The short, stocky fellow who rang her doorbell handed Della a Special Events Production card and introduced himself as "Rick, the production manager for her special evening."

Della asked, "Special evening?"

"Yes, we're here to create a special evening for you complete with a chef, clothes, props, and private entertainment courtesy of Edward Dawson."

"Really?" Della screeched. "All that?"

"Yes," Rick said. "Tonight is your night." Della was stunned. Without delay, Rick led his production crew in. They brought in tables, candles, drapes, drinks, rugs, and an enormous bouquet of wild orchids. It would be two hours before the musicians arrived and by then, Rick told Della, the penthouse would be transformed into a palace. Della was fitted by a personal stylist and decked in a white satin dress on the spot.

She tried to call Neilmore five times on her cell phone, but she had not picked up. This was not the type of occasion any woman should be forced to experience without giving her girl a preview. She left another message just before Edward rang the doorbell.

The company's professional host dressed in a black tuxedo seated Edward in Della's dining room that had been transformed from ordinary to a room fit for entertaining the Queen of Scotland. The crystal glasses, sparkling vases, and gold-leafed China atop the embroidered lace table cloth added to the elegant tone of Della's special evening. That's what it would be always: Della's Special Evening.

Edward was dressed in white. Della had never thought of a man being *radiant* until that night.

And then with the dimming of the lights and the arrival of a flutist-cellist duo, dinner was served. Salad first followed by a main course of crepe cheese potatoes, cream spinach, lobster, and prime rib. The champagne flutes stayed full of Dom Perignon. And they talked endlessly again amidst the perfect background music.

Della showed Edward pictures of her family. She wanted to impress him with all the travel photos but she rarely took them of just sights; most of them included the lovers along the way. Della did not want to explain the other men, she had already became talkative enough about David, who was on some resort playing golf with all the figures from City Hall. Edward didn't have any photographs to show Della. He said that he had plenty of pictures of his chalet in Stockholm that he wanted to share with her next time.

"Stockholm? I thought that was the one place you wanted to visit but hadn't yet been."

"Of course, I've been to Stockholm, Della. I sometimes live there. I get a little antsy, for obvious reasons, about sharing too much information too soon. But I'm here in your lovely home and I see from your antiques and fine taste in art—I love that original Keith Haring above the breakfast counter—you have excellent taste."

Della stiffened and sat upright. She wiped her mouth lightly. Edward reached across the table for well-manicured fingers, eyeing the sparkling rings snug around them. "What's the matter, Della?"

"I don't like dishonesty. Stockholm, a wife you haven't mentioned yet maybe, what else? It all comes from the same source of dishonesty." Based on Della's fiery response, Edward suspected she had been cheated on before or something just as detrimental. He should have given her more credit for remembering all the details from their previous conversation, including his slip-ups.

"I know. It was uncalled for on my part." Edward took out his wallet and showed Della what appeared to be a Swiss identification card. "You'll come with me here one day, Della, right?" He brushed her face delicately with his hand. She smiled slowly.

There was an uncomfortable pause. She didn't want to talk about Stockholm. "What is it that you really want, Edward? Do you want happiness, peace of mind, the occasional fling?"

"I don't know. I'm still trying to figure it out. What about you?"

Della didn't have to hesitate. "I want to retire early. I'm tired of working for someone else on their own terms. You paid a lot of money to be with me tonight and I'll tell you exactly what I want out of life. I think about my retirement. You'll probably say I'm too young and ambitious to focus on that, but it's true. My girlfriends dream about their wedding day: bridesmaids, the rings, a reception met by a thousand people, and riding their new husbands on the honeymoon bed. I dream about my retirement party, Edward." She sipped from the champagne glass perkily as if toasting herself.

Edward stared wildly at her. "Well, I dare say you are a very… colorful woman, Della. And you're right, I'm about to say you're too young and successful at what you do to think about retiring early. Will you make sure I at least get a condo in the Metropon?"

Della winced at hearing the magic word that took up most of her day. She had planned to get her hair rolled with Neilmore before the absurd emergency meeting was called. "What made you think of that, Edward? I'd rather not spoil the evening with conversation about work, even if you're joking."

"Sweet heart, I am certainly joking, but I can respect your work day when it is done. So, what kind of retirement party should I plan for you?" His smile was so charming, Della dismissed his gutsy request. She felt like an utter princess at the queen's ball. Had David ever existed? Della mused.

"I want it to be in the major ballroom of a big five-star hotel. I want a caravan of white limousines. All of them will be playing jazz. I want all of my friends and family to be dressed in white formal wear. I want balloons, streamers, singing and dancing all over the streets outside the hotel.

The room will be filled with orchids and roses. The highest point will be when I arrive to toast myself and break my glass and say goodbye to working for a corporation. My retirement is my own special glory. This is when my life will really begin!"

Edward could see that Della was quite tipsy now, riding the stream of a heartfelt goal, crazy as it sounded.

"What would your parents think?"

"Honey, my parents are very wealthy. They worked for every dime and retired together. They paid for an education that would allow me to work my butt off then take their chosen path. The only difference between me and them is that I plan on retiring alone." Edward took the first bite of the haystack mousse and licked the fork slowly. Della chuckled. "Are you listening to me?"

Indeed. Edward was hanging on every word that rolled off Della's sweet tongue. He even complied when she recited the fable her grandmother told her after church one day. It was the story of love.

There was a woman that came out of her house and saw three men with long, white beards sitting in the front yard. She did not recognize them. "I know we've never met, but you must be hungry. Please come in and have something to eat."

"Is the man of the house home?" they asked.

"No," she said, "he's out."

"Then we cannot come in," they replied.

In the evening when her husband came home, she told him what happened.

"Go tell them I am home and invite them in!"

The woman invited them in.

"We do not go into a house together," they replied.

"Why is that?" she asked.

"The old man patiently explained: "His name is Wealth." He pointed to one of his companions. Then to the other, he said, "He is Success and I am Love." Then he added, "Now go in and discuss with your husband what was said. Her husband was overjoyed.

"How nice!" he shouted. "Since that is the case, let us invite wealth. Entice him to come in so he can fill our house with weath!"

His wife disagreed. "My dear, why don't we invite Success?"

The couple's daughter-in-law was listening from other side of the house. She jumped in with her own suggestion: "Would it not be better to invite Love? Our house will be filled with Love!"

The woman stepped outside and approached the men. "Which one of you is Love?" Please come in and be our guest."

Love walked towards the entrance. The other two men got up to follow him. Surprised, the woman asked Wealth and Success, "I only invited Love. Why are you coming in?"

The old men replied together: "If you had invited Wealth, Success, the other two of us would have stayed out. However, since you invited Love, and whenever there is Love, there is also Wealth and Success. We must be permitted to enter."

At the conclusion, Edward sipped leisurely on his champagne. "I like that story."

"Are you just being a gentleman? You know, you're very good at it... almost too good." Della chuckled and took a bite out of her own piece of cake. She looked down at her tailored dress and thought herself to be a very lucky woman. Here and now, Della James was sprawled out on the lap of luxury. Edward Dawson epitomized the "playmate" she had always wanted. She had hoped to keep him ensnared for a long time.

"Della, tell me about your lady lawyer friends.

What are they like? Do you love them like sisters? Are they all in relationships?"

"Edward, you have a real curiosity about women, don't you? The way we feel, the way we make ourselves pretty in the morning, the way we attract men... or other women." In fact, Della had never met another man who was so preoccupied about the inner-workings of the opposite sex.

"Well, yes, I am intrigued. I like to know the woman I daydream about, what she thinks about, who she surrounds herself with. Is that so wrong?"

She didn't think it actually wrong, but she wasn't used to such probing. Della attracted men who fed off her aggression and her power. They usually had a grand time together, whether for two days or two weeks, and both were back on the hunt for the next exciting thrill. The short-term gratification resulted in more loneliness. Della knew this but her own patterns had a stranglehold on the way she lived her life.

"Edward, no, it's not wrong to want to know more about me. I'm very happy being the woman I am. And as you can see, I am *all* woman!" Della laughed at her own silliness while the host poured more champagne. She wondered how much this production had cost but didn't ask.

"I am not a desperate woman. I do know a lot

of women desperate for a relationship after going through a divorce from a man who didn't make them happy in the first place. They throw good judgment out the window because they don't enjoy being alone. They're so used to having a man around the house telling them what to do, they won't screen new prospects very well. If he looks good and has a job, they will move him in. It becomes a rush decision because they're downright lonely or bored." Della swayed gently in her seat to the Barry White tune playing.

"You must think I'm going too fast?" Edward closed his eyes and took in the music. Della wanted to dance, but was afraid she would slip as soon as she stood. The alcohol had hit her with force.

"That depends. What do you want from me?"

Edward reacted like Della had punched him in the jaw. "Ouch, that really hurts."

"Well, everybody is looking for something. Do you think you're going to sleep with me after this special production ends?"

"Della, what man wouldn't want to sleep with you? You're one of the most gorgeous ladies I have ever sat at the same table with. But that's not my game at all. I haven't even tried to kiss you."

Della contemplated his response. No, he had not even tried to kiss her. She found that to be strange.

What would he do if I planted one on him?, she thought. "Can I kiss you, Edward? You deserve it for giving me this lovely evening."

"Dance with me instead. You can have my lips another time. I want to see the way you move in that dress," he said thickly. Della put her glass down and honored the request. Edward helped her up and led her to the center of the living room. They moved effortlessly together.

"So, Della, what do you think of this evening?" Edward whispered.

"Well, I certainly didn't expect anything like this. What made you think to do this for me?"

"I like building memories, Della. I like being able to photograph special moments in my mind. It pleases me to pull one out of the photo box and know that I made that memory, no matter what the price of it was."

The night had come to a close and the production company cleaned up everything swiftly. Della and Edward shared a few more laughs before she asked him to help her out of the dress. "You don't need to be helped out of the dress," Edward said. "Matter of fact, sleep in it, it's yours to keep." Della had stood in the foyer filled with an unexplainable longing as Edward closed the front door behind him.

CHAPTER *Seven*

Joan and Terrence James were typical self-made millionaires. They didn't mind driving used cars, clipping grocery store coupons and driving the property value of their middleclass neighborhood up. If the adult James' didn't have but one credit card between them and wore Seikos instead of Rolexes, they hadn't spared any expense on their two daughters, on their home, on their traveling.

To look at Mr. and Mrs. James, you wouldn't guess they had been around the world twice. The routine scenario was Joan smiling over her spicy shrimp pasta and heavy helpings of Southern red velvet cake while Terrence tinkered in the garage among dusty antiques. And they both shared a knack for storytelling.

It was Neilmore who admired the pair most. She

loved sitting in Mrs. James' kitchen listening to her family tree tales over pans of strawberry batter and creamy icing. Mr. James would zoom through and add to the stories before filling up his water jug to exit again. Neilmore pretended they were her parents, easy as the sun fanning through the window, dancing across the China and crystal in aurora borealis prisms.

Neilmore had recorded all she knew about the James family in her journal. The diary was really a generic biography about them.

Della and Jamie grew up in the quiet Atlanta suburb of Dekalb where Mr. and Mrs. James were the first Black home owners. Neither of them had gone to college, but outliving Jim Crow and growing up Black in the South during the '50s was an education in itself.

Terrence was a budding realtor then, one of Atlanta's first Blacks in the business. There was something fundamental Neilmore couldn't exactly remember. It frustrated her that she didn't know if Terrence's grandfather had been a freed slave who owned a barbershop and later went into real estate and insurance. Or was it that Terrence's grandfather was a close alliance to an emancipated millionaire realtor? She put a big question mark in her journal. Either way, as Neilmore relayed to her sister in New York

excitedly, Terrence got into real estate because someone in his family or close to the family had been a
freed slave. That detail inspired Neilmore more than
the sculptures of Michelangelo.

Joan and Terrence met at a civil rights meeting,
registering to vote. Their names were still on the
roster of the first Black voters to register in that part
of the south. When Martin Luther King Jr. leant his
preaching voice to desegregate the South, you could
say they were already in the Ebenezer Baptist Church
"choir."

Joan took up collecting and restoring junk, making a business of it at first, before tapping into interior
design to complement Terrence's buying and refur-
bishing homes. As the couple expanded their businesses, they remained in the circle of well-respected
Black professionals. They were committed to what
was known as true "community-building."

The couple delighted in collecting indigenous art
from around the world to airports, museums and
public schools. They enjoyed heading educational
foundations and scholarship funds; endorsing social
change campaigns; being history-makers overall.
Yes, Neilmore, "The Reader," as Joan and Terrence
called her, was honored to sit in their kitchen and
hear their stories firsthand. In fact, she enjoyed their

company as much as she had enjoyed spending time with Della and Jamie.

Neilmore was accepted into the James' home as Della's Harvard sister and it gave Neilmore's heart pure joy to be appreciated and in their family for who she was—and not where she came from.

Neilmore's upbringing had not held the same signature privileges as Della's childhood. In fact, except for sharing an astute Harvard education, they were virtually from different planets. Neilmore's single mother struggled to make ends meet, which ultimately set the stage for the quality of their lives. There was undergrad school on full scholarship and the magna cum laude graduation party for two. Then Neilmore finished Ivy League grad school on advances and still worked side jobs as long as it took to pay off the hefty loans.

There were things about her mother that Neilmore cherished while sitting in Joan's kitchen. Lila died before she saw her only girl graduate from Harvard. She poured over the stove to make sure Neilmore had a four-course meal to eat at the law library each day. All the while, Lila sung gospel songs and listen to the morning news on the tiny television set. She wrote letters to distant relatives and friends from out of town every night at the kitchen counter. And whenever Neilmore was sick with the flu, Lila delivered a whole lemon meringue pie to her on a bed tray. Surely, the time and love it takes to put the right ingredients together to make a life or a good cake can be transferred from one kitchen to another.

Della and Jamie grew up in a three-story Victorian house in the Southbelt Heights section of Atlanta. When Della walked up to her front door, she landed on the porch beside Olmec planters brimming with colorful flowers representative of her family. The driveway was paved with red and gray octagon insets on a slant leading up to that very welcoming porch. The surrounding front yard bred huge magnolia trees that sheltered the white flowers in full bloom underneath. Once inside, visitors were greeted by high ceilings and a winding staircase of wrought iron with mahogany railings. Every room held extraordinary artifacts and antiques highlighted by personally appointed color schemes on the furniture and walls.

In contrast, the apartment Neilmore grew up in was bleak. When she lugged groceries up the five dingy flights of the apartment in New York City, Neilmore shared the distance with rats—the big ones only spotted around tenements. She never complained about their depressing surroundings since school and work took up most of her time anyway.

The cove that Mother and daughter shared was the lab where they worked dreams into reality.

CHAPTER *Eight*

Della faintly heard the door. Her response was delayed because the numbness in her body would not let her move right away. She could not get Edward's aliases out of her head or the photographs in Marlon's office that shot out a white flicker from his toothy smile. Della never felt so used or confused in her life. The knock got louder.

She looked in the peep hole and saw her sister with hands on hips and shaking her head side to side. "Open up, I know you are in there," said Jamie.

"I'm coming!" Della unlocked the door slowly.

"What took you so long?" Jamie's interrogating nature was like her husband's.

"I'm just completely worn down."

"What are you so tired from?" Jamie asked.

Della was surprised. "You mean your high and

mighty husband didn't tell you I sat in his office for nearly four hours gawking at a criminal boyfriend's mug shots two days ago, Della mused. How could she not know?

"Perhaps that's my business." Della's voice rose like it always did when Jamie got on her nerves. Usually it didn't take long.

"The way you are dragging around, it's like you've been drinking for days and your hangover's a mile wide." Jamie looked Della up and down. Her hair was way too unkempt and her robe was splashed with food—definitely not the Della she was used to being in the same room with. In contrast, Jamie was decked in an autumn suit with matching chocolate brown suede boots.

Della just smirked as Jamie huffed and went to the bathroom. The telephone rang. Della was afraid to pick it up, but figured Jamie would if she didn't. It was David, the on-again, off-again boyfriend.

"Where you been?" barked David." I've tried to contact you all weekend."

"Hmm, I was a little busy on a special case. Sort of a weekend study of a new client; I had to hole up for a while."

"What case?" David pressed on. "It's not like you to disappear like that. I got no telephone call and your car was in the driveway all weekend? Baby, you were with someone."

"Does it really matter to you, David? I was not into sitting around and watching sports."

"Who said you got to watch?"

"What, you don't trust me or something?" Della shouted. Jamie rounded the corner and listened to the dialogue intently. "You never listen to me anyway. Talking to you is like talking to a wall. Nothing happens."

Della shot a questioning stare at Jamie, wondering why she was so nosy, why she had even come by.

"That's how you feel, huh?" David fired back. "Listen to your animosity, Della. What is wrong with you?"

"Yes, that's how I feel, David. I spent the weekend without seeing you, so what? I had work to do and it comes first."

With that, David hung up the phone. Della couldn't remember the last time a man had slammed the phone down on her.

She anticipated a scathing lecture from Jamie. Like Neilmore, her sister had always been inquisitive about Della's love affairs. Perhaps since she had been intimate with Marlon first, there would always be tension. For the sake of their parents (and good old-fashioned karma, Grandma Sophonie would insist), Della made peace with her. Marlon was another story.

It came. "Well, what are you going to do? Keep David, the poor guy that you're tired of, or continue to date your new man?" Jamie obviously had no clue that Della was arrested. Neilmore swore secrecy when she picked her up at the station, but it was rather strange that Marlon had not said a word. Della was suspicious.

"Look, I've been with David for a while and I'm bored. Do you hear me? B-O-R-E-D."

"Quit him then. Stop being two-faced," Jamie shrugged. Della fell back on the couch and motioned for Jamie to sit down.

"Two-faced? Why do I have to be two-faced when I'm just exploring my options?"

"Look, Della, if the man has nothing to offer you and you are not in love, get out of the relationship. If not, you're both going to be really miserable down the road."

"Jamie, I did not ask for advice. I'm tired and I planned on being alone today.

On that note, please turn the ringer off before you leave. Besides, I've already paid my dues in life, in college and to you."

Jamie fidgeted with her dress before responding.

"I knew you were going to say something like that, Della Fran. I did not come over here to ruin your life or wreck your reclusive time. You're doing that all on your own. I really just came by to check on you. I saw Neilmore at the French café down the street this morning, and she acted strange every time I asked a question about you. I wanted to make sure you were all right."

"I appreciate you coming by and I appreciate your concern." Della's words were sincere.

Jamie smiled brightly. You would have thought she was kissed by an angel. "You really appreciate my visit?"

"Sure, I do. Jamie, as I get older I understand myself better. I'm starting to learn the difference between happiness and heartache. To resist your popping in unannounced would cause more heartache. We'd get in a lengthy discussion about why I want to be alone, then you'd curse and stomp, demand that I give up the boring boyfriend and I'd be more exhausted." After a long pause, they both chuckled.

"Let's not talk about happiness. I know Neilmore would be on the telephone all day, just trying to capture the *thought* of being happy!" Jamie stood up and blew a kiss to Della, who was now under her down comforter. Neilmore remembered to turn off the ringer before locking the door behind her.

Della contemplated catching up on her house-work, especially the laundry that was now falling out of two hallway closets. She thought about what Jamie had said. The comment about her being two-faced bothered her. After all, it was she who spent money in the relationship with David, she who initi-ated all the fun, she who pretended to love basket-ball and football when he needed someone to cheer with or drool on when his favorite player scored. Della finally asked herself why loneliness was such a fear of hers.

Perhaps that fear catapulted her into the mess with Edward... or whoever the man was with the beautiful hands.

CHAPTER *Nine*

"Jamie, don't you have a key?" Della's shout came from the couch. She was irritated by another knock on the door that disturbed her solitude. Della didn't bother peeping through the hole before opening the door to find Neilmore there.

"Girl, I thought you were my nagging sistà again."

"Well, I am her! Just the other one who's not blood related." Della gently tugged her inside the door. It occurred to her that these days with the Feds possibly turning over every leaf to look for their madman, she should take precaution before opening the door. The thought of her place being stalked sickened Della.

Neilmore said she had run into Jamie in the parking lot. Della rolled her eyes, imagining what the pair had discussed. Anything but Edward was acceptable, she supposed. "Look, I don't want to talk about Edward. I've not heard from the dog and I have no idea what the authorities' next move is. I'm trying to relax while I can."

"Is that the proper way to greet the one who bailed you out of that hellhole? Besides, I was stopping through to see if you wanted to go to lunch. I've been dying to try out that new Asian fusion place in Midtown."

Della was glad that Neilmore finally wanted to eat out after tucking so many pennies away, but she refused to get up from the couch. "Let's do it another day."

"Fine, so what is going on with David?"

Della could not believe her ears. She wondered if the two most important women in her life cared about something as much as they did her love life. It was getting ridiculous. "Neilmore, I don't know yet. That's exactly what I was contemplating before you popped over. Whatever Jamie told you is probably all there is to know."

Neilmore couldn't help but think, *Della's not exactly the poster child for naïve but she sure is a good runner-up.*

It was spring break or something. Neilmore couldn't remember when exactly. One of those times

Della dragged her home to Atlanta to *hang around the house*. They were all in the James' living room, stretched out on the couches, sprawled on the floor hugging pillows, propped on Joan's favorite piece, the fuchsia silk divan. The Black Forest Chocolate Cakes—Neilmore, Marlon and Jamie—against Ms. Angelfood Cake, Della.

They were laughing at Della for saying, "I am not color-struck. Look around this room. How could I be?" The more Della pleaded her case, the harder they had laughed.

Marlon said, "No, Della. You're not color-struck on the outside. You're color-struck on the inside and that's where you're pure green."

"I know you can't be mad at a sister for having the wherewithal to do what she pleases, when she pleases, however she pleases?" Della asked Marlon.

"No, I ain't mad at you all. But don't you ever get tired of being a *material girl*? Buying and disposing of things, even people, once they fail to satisfy your impulsive shopping spree of the moment?"

Della had waved Marlon on. "Get a life. I don't see my life as one long impulsive shopping spree for your information. If what y'all trying to get is all this *buy Black, be Black* all the time stuff, I can't help it if my world is bigger than the *community* and if my..."

Marlon started and Neilmore and Jamie had pitched in with pleasure. "Sixteen days in Rome with Gregorio."

"Thirty days in Tribeca with Zena, painting New York red."

The more places and names on Della's long list of brief interludes with lovers they threw, the harder they laughed. Della's cheeks and ears turned rose pink.

"Y'all are really bad, you know that? I see not one of y'all has the decency to remember summer in Dakar with Aziz?"

Neilmore stepped in to defend Della. "Della, we're not mad at you for doing your thing. It's just that there is so much more that you personally bring to the table, more than your money." Neilmore got on her legacy-of-Southern-Blacks soapbox for a minute and then stepped off it, saying, "Della, you are so much richer than you show the world, and I guess we all wish you'd share more of yourself. You are so smart. You are so beautiful. You are so…"

"Such a freak!" Jamie jumped in and turned things nasty. "You are too stupid to know that you are just amusement for all these folks. You're the international lover, huh? Their exotic plaything. You are so hooked on yourself, you can't see what people around you really think of you."

Despite Neilmore and Marlon's pleading for Jamie "not to go there," she went. Della was stunned. "Get it out your system, Jamie. Go ahead. I know you've wanted to get it off your D-cups for awhile. Shoot."

And Jamie did. She told Della she should ride her little planet for as long as she could because she was willing to bet good money someone out there was not going to be taken for granted and shoved off to the side just because Della wanted it that way. One day, someone would surely bring Della's little planet crashing down. Jamie could bet on it.

"Well, *Ms. Always in the Shadows*, you sure stepped way outside your shy bag today. Thanks for showing me *your* true colors."

Joan and Terrence had come home from the grocery store and everyone rushed to help them bring in bags from the car. Everyone but Della. She had been completely stung by Jamie's vindictive words.

Neilmore loved both Jamie and Della, but she was acutely aware of Jamie's potentially cruel side. Even when Jamie was happy, her eyes burned with something unpleasant. She was afraid for Della, but she didn't want to tell her, as Neilmore remembered the past.

"Della, I'm going to check out the Luther Vandross concert at the Woodruff tonight. Do you want to come?"

Della reached for her friend's hand and held it tight. They were linked by years of friendship and that Della would always hold dear, but she just wanted to be alone with her thoughts. "Why is it so hard for the world to understand the meaning of solitude? Am I a hardened criminal to want it from time to time? Do you know how it feels to be used by a con artist? To be stripped of a strong ego by a charming, handsome stranger who doesn't care about you?"

Neilmore took her time before responding to Della's outburst. "I don't think anyone can tear that ego apart! It's just bruised temporarily. They'll find this guy 'Edward' and you'll continue breaking hearts all over the world just as before." She was only half joking and they both knew it.

Della continued holding Neilmore's hand as she had done so many times before on that couch, in the midst of sisterly conversation. Except this time, it wasn't about Neilmore's punctured heart. "Della, I'm not going to sit here and lecture you about your lack of common sense for the millionth time since we've known each other. I came to get you out of the house. Besides, you love Luther's music!"

Yes, she did love Luther Vandross. Even Edward knew it. One day, he had sent a package to her door filled with every CD Luther had made. Neilmore knew Della was reflecting on that day, the same one Edward had rented out a hotel suite at The W in celebration of her settling a case.

"Will it help for you to talk about him? You only revealed his lavish-as-I-wanna-be side, Della. Didn't you have a clue that he was a criminal?" Neilmore's frank words penetrated Della.

She couldn't decide whether to lash out at her for the question or beat herself up for being so naïve. There was a part of her that had always suspected something. No man could be that generous and be absolutely sane. For the sake of their friendship—and a good laugh—Della finally disclosed more information about Edward and his imaginative ideas about "dating."

CHAPTER *Ten*

The day after the production company transformed Della's house into a five-star restaurant, Edward had sent a white limousine to pick her up for a picnic.

"Della, it's good that we live in America because we have an opportunity to learn a lot about life and living. That is what makes this country so terrific. Everything has value because we live in a material world and it has its purpose. We may not agree with its purpose or like its value. Somehow everything ties into the function of this world, don't you agree?" Edward said it while in the warm park.

Eyes covered with dark glasses, Della fidgeted with the drawstring on her pants. She had listened to Edward for a long time before speaking, and the sun was getting to her. "I understand, Edward, but this sounds like an economics seminar. Would you like to pack up the food and take a walk?" Della didn't admit she had woken up with a throbbing headache from all the champagne. She couldn't refuse getting outside for a little while, but she wasn't sure what Edward was hinting at.

"Della, what I mean is that everyone needs a partner. Whether in business or in love, we all benefit from teamwork," Edward continued. "I guess... I guess what I really want to know is if my options with you are open."

The ducks in the pond weren't close enough for Della to focus on. She took in the marvelous magnolia trees instead. Della was not ready for this conversation.

"Edward, you've already whisked me into events that aren't normal on the dating scale. I've only known you for a few weeks. I am very attracted to you and I enjoy your company, but... can we save the questions for another time? Thank you for being honest, but now is not the time for pinning down my intentions... I can't predict anything right now."

Edward responded without hesitation: "Della, to me, time has value. The older I get the more I realize I can't magically create time. You never know when it is your last hour... or your last moment. As the cliché goes, 'here today, gone tomorrow.'" Picking up on the signal that Della's mouth was sealed for the time being, he agreed to walk around the pond. "Can I hold your hand?" he asked, while helping her off the blanket.

The gesture reminded Della of seventh grade when Timothy Russell had shyly asked her to dance. She smiled sweetly and kissed Edward on the cheek.

As the sun began to set the lights from the city begin to glisten and glitter. The night remained warm and no one was in the park except them.

Little did Della know that before she could fully recover from the evening's glitz, Edward was up to more grandeur. Della was given the key to Edward's master suite on the twentieth floor of The Waldroff downtown. When she stepped into the spacious room, Edward was nowhere to be found.

Della surveyed her surroundings: a regency stained beech chaise lounge formally ebonized, a Victorian writing table with kingwood cross-banding and a kidney-shaped top with tooled leather panels. And on the mantle there was a French terracotta sculpture of the Contessa de Sabran on variegated marble. She could spot luxury miles away.

As Della stepped onto the balcony, the phone rang. It was Edward. "Della, I want you to go into the bedroom and pick the evening gown you would like to wear tonight. I brought three evening gowns with matching handbags and shoes. I know that they will fit you." He didn't say goodbye before hanging up.

Della chose the Yves Saint Laurent white gown with the gold handbag and shoes. She bathed and got dressed, not knowing what to anticipate. Edward called an hour later and said that he was waiting in the lobby. He wore a black tuxedo. Again, Della was whisked away in a limousine.

"So, how do you feel today, beautiful Della?" Edward asked and kissed her cheek delicately.

"I'm still enjoying the effects of last evening. Don't you let a woman catch her breath? You surprised me again."

"I read in the paper that the Metropon deal was finalized. Your name was bold-faced in the announcement. I thought to myself, *that Della James is a woman who gets what she wants, and she deserves every ounce of it*. I wanted to treat you to a celebration."

"Yes, it's true. Case closed, but after last night, perhaps I should be treating you to dinner." Della pulled out a Gold Discover card from the handbag and flashed a smile. Edward gestured for her to put it away.

"Nonsense, I don't mind forking over cash to make a special lady happy. I don't care about money."

What with the sleek hotel suite, rented limousines everyday and new dresses, *obviously* the man did not care about racking up the bills to impress a lady. Della decided to enjoy herself two nights in a row and forgo the questions.

"How do you like the limousine, Della? We're going about thirty minutes outside of town, so have a drink if you'd like. I told the driver to stock up on your favorite whiskey."

"Edward, you really act like you've known me for years, treating me like we've shared several honeymoons. Of course I like the limo, especially the soft tan leather seats and the moon roof. This is a beautiful night for a date," Della sat back and relaxed against Edward.

"I told you, this is not a date, it's a celebration in honor of Della James." He stared at Della's luscious lips as if wanting to devour them, then turned to the window. "Most ladies feel elegant when they're in a limousine and I'm sure you're no different."

Della chose her words carefully and distanced herself a few inches. "Please do not insinuate I'm like all other women. I guess that's what you've seen on television." For a split second, she thought about instructing the driver to take her home.

"Della, you're right. You're not like any woman I've met. And to tell you the truth, if this all seems strange, it's because I know you have a hundred men chasing you and I want to stand out. I think of no one but you. How does that make you feel? Does that frighten you?"

She wasn't sure what to respond to first. The hundred men that were actually *not* chasing her or the declaration of his feelings. "I'm flattered, but please know that you already have my attention. You don't have to keep outdoing yourself with all the glamour. By the way, how did you know my dress size?" Della poured herself a whiskey and sour.

Edward seemed flushed for a moment. "I guessed your size. As for your attention, whatever happened to David?"

So, men did feel threatened by other men after all. Della had guessed that side of romance to be a chick thing. "David is still in the horizon until I figure out how close I want him. All my friends think he is the one for me because he's stable and hardworking, wealthy and handsome."

"Sounds like a good package to me," Edward responded. As she turned to him, he surprised Della with a kiss. Soaked with desire, his tongue gently kissed at Della's lips. Her whole body shivered with pleasure. Just as she was dropping her handbag to wrap her arms around him, Edward pulled away abruptly. His face flattened like the kiss had never happened.

"Are you afraid of women, Edward? Were you the type of boy that didn't get kissed until the baby-sitter planted one on you? Did you leave the party when a naughty game of truth or dare started?" Della was sick of playing shy girl. She was used to assertive men who only got bolder with the second kiss. She started to wonder if Edward was secretly gay. It didn't make sense with his pursuit of her, but Della had never experienced such an enigmatic man. She should have guessed then that something was entirely off about Edward Dawson.

"You want me to rip that dress off and take you in this limo, don't you? Is that how you're used to being treated? Well, maybe we should say goodbye if that's the case. My mother taught me better." Edward did not blink while gazing into Della's eyes. She was dumbfounded.

"I'm sorry if I offended you, Edward." It was a dull response, but it's all Della could give in that instant. Before she knew it, Edward was holding her hand again. They already seemed like a couple.

The limo arrived at The Nines, a restaurant tucked in the back of another five-star hotel. The entrance to the restaurant was a bridge over a lake with a trickling waterfall filled with tropical flowers and birds.

Della had dined in too many restaurants to count in Atlanta, but she never knew this one existed. They walked through the lobby of the hotel, through the restaurant and into a private room behind a crystal door trimmed in oak. The room had one center table with candlelight and a white baby grand piano in the rear of the room. The lights dimmed as soon as they sat down and a romantic voice emanated from the piano singing a sweet love song.

Swordfish drowned in clam sauce was served with a host of vegetables. A bottle of Dom Perignon came in a diamond cooler alongside a small velvet box. "This is for your most recent achievement, dear Della." Edward presented the box. Inside was a pair of diamond earrings. Della didn't make a move, but stared at the jewelry in a daze.

"Diamonds are forever and so is success once you taste it. These are to remind you."

Della accepted the present with a kiss across the candlelit table. In that moment, she felt deep compassion for Edward Dawson. The kind of feelings that don't last beyond the moment, but when they're felt, the intense affection swells the heart with sweet joy and appreciation.

They ate in silence. After dinner, Della and Edward went to the main ballroom where Edward was invited to sing to Della. She learned something new on this night, as his voice was terrific and sultry. He sung a beautiful ballad by Julio Iglesias, "Can't Help Falling in Love."

After dancing for an hour, Della asked to go back to The Waldroff Hotel. She mentioned having a mild headache, so Edward summoned a concierge for someone to give them both back and foot massages. After the massage, Edward told Della, "This is your evening, spend the night in my suite and I'll call you tomorrow." She didn't have a chance to respond before he was out the door. Della had no idea where he went. Once undressed, she fell fast asleep on the bed.

Della had slept through the morning and into the afternoon at the hotel. A message had been left to call the limousine company once she was ready to go home. Edward had not returned.

While Della was asleep, her mind traveled back to when she was a child. Jamie had been with her in a dress shop. The shop's owner asked the girls if they had dates for the prom. Della said, "Of course not. My parents will not allow me to date until I turn seventeen." Miss Sally dropped the subject and proceeded to the back of the shop to bring out the gowns. The sisters waited anxiously.

"I want you girls to try on the dresses to make

sure they fit properly." Della was the first to sway in the mirror with the remarkable, shimmering fabric. She smiled ear to ear while Jamie frowned at her. Miss Sally cooed at Della as Jamie stood there without making a move for her own gown.

As Della had turned and turned in front of the mirror, the bottom of the gown was suddenly on fire. Jamie was on her knees lighting the fabric with a match, laughing and rocking back and forth. Della had screamed in astonishment, the flames almost licking her skin.

Before the nightmare got worse, Della opened her eyes and realized she was right where Edward had left her the previous evening—a far cry from being engulfed in flames at a dress shop by her older sister. She fixed herself a cup of coffee and sat on the balcony before calling the limousine company. Edward was honestly making her feel like every day was a vacation.

When Della stepped into the backseat of the limousine, Edward was sitting there with a lush bouquet. "Hello beautiful Della. Did you sleep until your heart was content?" He was dressed in the pilot uniform she had not seen since the day they met.

"Yes, really I did I guess. I can't believe it's mid-afternoon. Are you leaving town?" Della was at a loss for words. Wondering why Edward hadn't mentioned his schedule, she felt insecure about their interaction suddenly. She couldn't possibly let herself get attached to someone so evasive. On the other hand, did she even have a right to know where he was going?

"I wanted to say goodbye before flying to France. I'll be gone for a little while. I'll call you once I get back." He smoothed her loose hair back and squeezed her knee. Della didn't respond but rubbed both of her eyes sleepily. Still a bit shaken by the nightmare, she didn't know what to say.

"What's the matter? We'll play some more the hour I return."

"It's just that I feel a little out of my element. You spoil me without notice, cart me around in one limousine after another, all the while never revealing much about yourself. I guess I'd really like to know more, and the mystery is starting to really disappoint me rather than intrigue me."

"Look," Edward said, " my sister is very sick and she's staying in a chalet alone. She's been writing a play for the last month. Last night she said that some of the locals had come down with a terrible case of bronchitis, and she's convinced she's come down with it. She's deathly afraid of hospitals and begged me to come," Edward said. The story came out in a gush. Della had a feeling that Edward was lying, but she didn't ask any questions. He had never revealed even having a sister.

Della was taken by a wave of emotion and began crying. She couldn't explain where the sadness had come from, but it was surely there. Was this all part of the hangover? Startled, Edward put his arm around Della and pulled her body into him.

"I think my sister hates me," Della confessed.

"I can't imagine that. You've only told me good things about Jamie." She was again surprised by his memory about the people in her life.

"Well, I think it's true, Edward. Maybe people are right about me being so self-absorbed that I don't see how I hurt people around me. I think my sister is one of those people."

"Why?" He rubbed her back like a soothing brother.

"Well, when I really think about it, she's the oldest, four years older. She's dark-skinned. Very pretty mahogany woman, but I'm not dark by anyone's standards. She's reserved. I'm not. And, well, when I think about it, I think she feels that I've stolen her light just because I'm who I am and as crazy as it probably sounds to a man, I think it's because I'm light-skinned."

Edward let out a thunderous laugh. In fact, Della had never heard him laugh like that before. "I beg your pardon?" She tried to free herself, but Edward pulled her in closer.

"Della, sometimes we worry about the silliest things, don't we? I'm here to tell you that your sister doesn't give a damn about your skin color. Furthermore, you're *both* very beautiful women."

This time Della did pull free and she sat up stiffly. "How in the world would you know what she cares about, Edward? She's had in it for me since I kissed her high school sweetheart."

As the limousine stopped in front of Della's building, the driver opened up the door. "Madam, may I hold your flowers?" She waited for Edward's response before turning to the driver.

Edward had not answered Della's inquiry. He kissed her on the cheek and said goodbye.

CHAPTER *Eleven*

"Della, I think you need to make another appointment with Dr. Venus," Neilmore finally spoke after listening to Della's follies for two hours. "You may be all right today, but this is only the beginning of what may come because of Edward. He has obviously played you for a head case. I'm afraid you will turn into one after it's all said and done!"

Della pulled the comforter over her head like a troubled little girl. "Do you really think I'm a head case, Neilmore? I don't feel like being scorned by that woman anytime soon."

"Della Frank, 'that woman' is brilliant. She knows what she's doing. She's been a doctor for over twenty…" Della cut her off with a hand barging out from underneath the cover.

"Please don't say anymore about 'the doctor.' Besides, I'm thinking about going away for a couple of days after working this week. I want the serenity of the beach, something to clear my head. Oh, a new attorney is joining the firm. Finally, another woman. Can you believe it?" Della figured Neilmore would comment about Wanda having more competition, but it was obvious that mystery man was now the hot topic.

"Della, do you really think the Feds will let you leave Atlanta?"

"Neilmore, I have not seen Edward in weeks. I know nothing. They have the car. I can't imagine what else I can give them as evidence. He was really very good about keeping his identity entirely concealed."

Neilmore shook her head in frustration. She was convinced that Della could come up with something she could give the authorities, but perhaps she was too shaken up to think straight. "Look, Della, I really believe if you can pull a little more information from that head of yours, they'll leave you alone and you can get back to your life. If you don't willingly connect with them, I'm afraid your life may be ruined. As a matter of fact, I just know it will. Please try to remember something concrete."

Della kicked her legs over the couch and paced the room. As frustrated as she was, she knew Neilmore was right. Her career was completely in jeopardy if she didn't cooperate. Della cringed at the thought of being plastered all over the newspapers for being conned by a man. She wouldn't and couldn't let that happen. At this point, only Neilmore and Marlon knew about the ordeal.

Neilmore swung off her heels and padded into the kitchen to make a pot of Della's favorite tea, the kind with super mental boosters. She was determined to help save the only real friend she had ever known. For hours, Neilmore probed Della about all her meetings with Edward. She listened to all the details, even wrote some notes down like a detective.

Della had not heard from Edward for two weeks after he claimed he was going to France to take care of his sister, the playwright. When he returned he asked her to breakfast and chauffeured her to a nice restaurant by a lake. The restaurant was a New England-style café with copper pans on the walls. The aroma of eggs filled the air.

Edward wanted to sit by the window because he knew that if they ran out of conversation, at least they would have the water ripples and the ducks to talk about. By this time, they had talked about so much, Della didn't want to talk any longer. Apparently, he didn't like the movies or the theatre because every time she mentioned them, Edward stared at her blank-faced. He never referred to many books although he was quite good at philosophizing everything. Yep, travel and food were high on the topic list but Della's career had always come first.

"I have told you all I want you to know about tort cases, summary judgments, and my feelings about being a real estate lawyer. I have told you what it means to be in the 'in' crowd of the legal community, all about my family, all about my education. I need to know more about you." The thoughts were boiling in her mind until she just asked him. "Edward, tell me more about your work. Somehow I missed the fine points about how you got started in the business."

"Well, Della, I can't tell you everything. It is just too much to talk about. Your work is more interesting. Aren't you involved in a litigation of a nuclear landfill in Nevada? And if your side wins, Cavengah Waste Management will go public on the New York Stock Exchange?"

"Yes, it's all true. It never ceases to amaze me. You leave for weeks, but you know everything about me as if we were living under the same roof. How is that, Edward?"

"Della, your firm is always mentioned in the papers. I care about you and what your future holds."

Huge plates of omelets, sausage and potatoes O'Brien were served in minutes. Della wondered if the food had come out of the microwave. "No, sweet darling, this place is far more refined. I ordered ahead of time for us."

"Do you ever worry about getting into a plane crash?" Della was not going to let up this time. She was really falling for Edward, and she was determined to know what the man was about before breaking it off with David.

"No. I know it can happen but I never think about it. Your chances of getting in an accident are more likely on a public street than a plane. I can't wait to fly just to get out of traffic. Traffic in each major city in America is horrible. Della, have you ever stayed in New York City for long? It is a madhouse there. Try getting a cab in Manhattan after 3:00 p.m. They are bumper to bumper. You can be stuck in the same spot for three hours and never move an inch. When I fly I may see a few aircraft on the runway. When I'm in the sky I don't see a bird that high, all I see is white cloud formations. That's it."

"So what interested you in flying in the first place?"

"I always watched the sky as a little boy in my small town."

"What town was that?"

"I'm not going to tell you that."

"Why not?"

"I'll tell you about my town a little later."

"Later, why later? What is it about your town that you don't want me to know?"

"Nothing, really. It's just a small, desolate town."

"It must be special." Della tore into her food while waiting on an answer with substance. She silently contemplated never seeing him again during that empty conversation. The "secrets" had been limitless. The problem was that Della had become powerfully attracted to him. They had not slept together, but her imagination had already run wild about the things she would do once it felt absolutely right.

"Della, I'm from the island of Jamaica."

"Jamaica! Are you a citizen of the United States? Do you have a green card? I knew there was something about you that I could not put my finger on."

"Excuse me? I do have my citizenship in this country. Please lower your voice." Edward looked at Della as if she were an annoying five year old. "I've had it for about ten years."

"Did you apply for it or did you marry someone then get a divorce?"

"What I have is dual citizenship."

Edward finally had knowledge of the law that she did not. Della did not mind learning something new. "I'm not very familiar with international law and citizenship."

Edward flashed a smile and relaxed. "Yes, you can do that. I like being international. Being international broadens your horizons. Some people are scared of travel and they won't leave the twelve-mile radius from their house. They live and die without ever seeing anything. I can't connect with that." Finally, Edward carried on about something other than her career and Della listened. She only opened her mouth to take another bite of food.

"The island is beautiful with white sands, aqua blue water, warm winds, palm trees, and water falls everywhere you turn. The tourists have taken over the best parts of the island and we must cater to them for work. I hate it. The tourists are sometimes nasty and they want you to take their demands. My country's national policy is to be nice to tourists, even at the expense of self-respect. This bothers me. I don't mind visitors because I like to visit beautiful places too, but I don't want to be exploited."

Della looked dismayed. "Do you have to be exploited, Edward?"

"If you only knew."

"Only knew what?"

"It is almost impossible to make it off the island without sponsorship. If you are too old that is. You are locked in for life unless you have children and family elsewhere. I don't mean to paint a bleak picture, but that's how it is to me. All except for my home. I can't wait for you to see it, Della."

And he raved about the grasslands and rain forests. He talked about a small ship that he sailed into the lagoon off Montego Bay. When Edward got far enough out into the lagoon, he would dive in the water and swim as deep as he could. He was no professional scuba diver, he reminded Della. He had no need for gear because his water was his home. The world of underwater creatures, the world of purple and yellow coral reef dynasties, large rocks and hidden caves. The only thing he liked better than swimming the lagoon during the day was swimming it at night.

"Are you serious?" Della asked, amazed.

Edward explained how at ease he'd be diving at night. A night dive into the Caribbean was the ultimate adventure. Della would have to be a guest in his vacation home whenever she could free herself from her caseload to come. That's right, she would never know it was night after she submerged herself into the water.

Della wasn't sure about all that, but Edward assured her the night light from the boat would gleam and reflect down in the water as would the moon.

He would be there with Della when she witnessed this magnificent sight.

Edward said that he had always wanted someone to appreciate the mystery of the ocean as he did. Della would be safe and she'd love it, he could tell. Della had looked at Edward's hands and imagined them parting clear blue Caribbean water. The idea of visiting his home in Montego Bay had sounded better by the minute. Then his tone changed again.

Edward had gone on about tourists taking over the island. She wasn't sure how to take her handsome prince now. Della found his hang-up to be incredibly narrow-minded. After all, she had been a tourist in dozens of countries and would continue to travel until she was old and decrepit. "So, what are you going to do with the rest of your day?" She changed the subject without grace or the usual transitions.

Edward folded his hands and thought real hard. Della waited patiently like an algebra teacher at the chalkboard. "I'm going to find out what brings you joy and rich excitement. What does it take to bring out the best in you? I'm going to find out and I'm going to do it soon."

"What in the world are you talking about, Edward? You've done it already. You've spent so much money on me, it's unreal. I'm not sure what you expect from me. Maybe it's time for you to say so."

"Sweetheart, most people don't know what they really want. That is the problem. Many times what a person wants is not available to them. If you can't control your desires and learn to be content, you will never be happy. You will never have peace of mind. And peace of mind means everything. Let me ask you a simple question: What nation in the world is the strongest nation? Is it the United States, China, or the Soviet Union?"

"I think it is the United States."

Just then the check had come and Edward nicely asked Della to pay the bill. He had forgotten his wallet at the hotel. She did not mind paying for one measly breakfast.

That day, Edward had said the strongest nation was actually the imagination. He pointed out that when a people could go free and be allowed to use their imaginations limitlessly, anything could happen. He was right. He had imagined a plot to con Della James and he had succeeded. When Edward called later, Della was still looking for her copy of the credit card bill she paid at the restaurant to add it to other receipts for her bookkeeper. She never found it.

Neilmore was so captivated by Della's stories, she was wrapped up in her own comforter on Della's big leather couch. While her friend was probably in more trouble than they could measure at this time, Neilmore secretly liked hearing about the crazy adventures. To this day, she had only dated a few men during her time in Atlanta and two of them were in the medical field. She enjoyed being single but wanted children by the time she was thirty-five or so. At thirty-three, Neilmore wasn't sure if she would meet that goal.

"Della, did he mention his parents at all, any children?"

Perhaps Neilmore's probing did help after all. "That dog snagged my signature when he gave me a 'get well' card for his mother to sign. I didn't know her, but he said he'd mentioned me and wanted us to eventually meet."

Edward had pulled out the card the day they had breakfast. She even read the endearing message he wrote and was impressed by the gesture. Della had thought nothing of signing the card. Perhaps that was a stupid mistake, but who would think they were signing all their financial information away to someone who treated them so romantically and asked for nothing in return? Della punched the pillow in retaliation. Neilmore gently grabbed her fist.

"Get to the Lexus, girl. You know we've all been dying to hear about that one."

"Oh, you and the crew? Neilmore, I told you that I don't want my family knowing about the arrest or the investigation. My parents would never forgive me! Marlon just happens to be on the case. I asked him not to tell Jamie, and he promised not to as long as they found him quickly. Otherwise, the story will have to go to the press in hopes that someone will turn him in."

CHAPTER Twelve

HOLIDAY SEASON

Edward had called one Saturday morning after another two weeks of absence. Della never refused to meet him. In fact, she was getting used to the thrill of being swept away somewhere mysterious and opulent. It seemed like his life was just one big luxurious affair. She wondered if Edward was keeping someone like her around in another part of the country. His patterns were too strange.

"I need to take care of some personal business this morning, then I'd like to go shopping. I'm going to a car dealer, and I'd like for you to come with me."

As Della didn't have anything planned that day and David was out of town, she agreed. "Della, what kind of car would be your dream automobile?"

"Oh, definitely a Lexus; they're sleek and powerful without all the conspicuous gadgets. I can't stand all the pimp ridin' souped up stuff." They laughed and Edward said he'd be there in thirty minutes to go to a Lexus dealer.

"What? You are going there just because I said it? That's crazy, Edward!"

"No, dear Della, I'm not going because you said it, promise. Luxury cars are my thing, too."

An hour after stopping to get bagels and coffee, they were on their way to a car dealership outside of town. Della wasn't familiar with the west side of town and glad not to be. Half of the area looked like war-torn Beirut. They pulled into the dealership, and Edward asked Della to stay in the car while he chatted with the manager. "I'm acquainted with him, and I'd like to butter him up before I show you off as the queen of diamonds card. I'd like to secure a deal today because I'll be spending more time in Atlanta in the coming months. Would you like that, Della?" Before she could answer, he kissed her hand and left for twenty minutes.

Edward led her out of the Towncar he was driving and into the salesman's office. "Sir, this is Della James."

The wiry old man gawked at her like a hungry predator. "I'm very glad to meet you, Ms. James.

You're one of the most beautiful women I have ever seen."

"Well, that's very nice of you. Thank you." Della was gracious, but a little uncomfortable with the scenario. Edward then pointed to a sparkling white Lexus and asked Della for her opinion. "Do you think this vehicle would suit my good looks and voracious appetite for the open road?"

"Hmm, well, if you put it that way, I thought you didn't care to drive very much? But, yes it's a beautiful car, probably very fast, too." Della stared at Edward questioningly while the old man still inspected her up and down.

"That's all I need to know, honey. I'll meet you back at the car if you don't mind," he replied.

Della went back to the car without saying goodbye to the salesman. The whole scene had been peculiar, but then again, nothing had been all that blasé with Edward Dawson.

Della had watched the two interact for a few minutes before the man gave Edward a set of keys. He returned swiftly.

"It was nice, wasn't it?"

"Well, are you going to get it?" Della asked.

"Oh, I don't know. I like Porsches too! We don't have time to look right now."

His demeanor had been a little freaky, but considering the money Edward had spent on Della the last six weeks, she dismissed any funny feelings about the morning. She shifted the conversation to what he had said about spending more time in Atlanta.

"So, you'll be staying here for a while this time?" Della blurted out.

"You would like that, wouldn't you? It depends on my job, really. I can't decide whether to go back to Jamaica for a while or make my home here and ask you to marry me." Edward did not flinch while delivering the statement. Astonished, Della covered her mouth with both hands. "Della, I was joking. We have imperative things to tend to before that happens." She did not respond to the bizarre assumptions, his unfeigned confidence that she would actually marry him.

The following day, Edward had told Della to be outside within the next hour. Low and behold, the new white Lexus had pulled up alongside the curb, and Edward sprang out of the driver's side. She could not believe her eyes. "Just say you like it or love it, and it's yours, Della."

"I love it!" And with Della's response, they were on the road driving for hours. Feeling rather intimate and high on being treated like a goddess, she had asked Edward some risky questions that day about money. He still didn't give any solid information about his status. Then again, Della had been so caught up in the events unfolding, she didn't care about being sharp as a tack (as Grandma Sophonie would insist when it came to men).

"Neilmore, I acted like a spoiled, power-driven bitch and I'm going to pay for it," Della confessed. "You know I could have bought that car with my own money if I really wanted it, but I let myself become a dependent, whiny brat for that man. Why, I ask you?"

Sipping from her tea, Neilmore was at a loss for words. She was engrossed in Della's dramatic story and didn't have any intention of characterizing her friend any differently than she already had for the last ten years. "Della, I'm not here to judge you, I'm here to love you and help you. What else happened? It seems like so much went on that you didn't tell your sista friend!"

Della snuggled up to Neilmore and continued with the tales, one detail after another.

Edward instructed Della to drive to Piedmont Park, where he had actually proposed to her. He had pulled a 3 karet ring out of his pocket while they sat next to the pond. Della remembered watching the in-line skaters jamming to some old hip hop tunes, and she had felt like fleeing into the crowd. At least that had been her initial reaction. "Della, I want you to consider marrying me. You don't have to answer today or even this month. I just feel like time is precious and I know you're the one for me."

"Look, I'm very attracted to you, Edward but I can't call this love. You're so mysterious, are you living another life? Do you feel like you can buy me with a shiny, new car? What's your dark side like? How do you deal with anger or the things that you don't get when you want them? Do you sleep naked, on the right or the left side?"

Edward grinned in a daze. He carefully put the ring back in his pocket and said that she could take her time. "Listen, don't sweat this. The car is yours. I like to do nice things for the people in my life. Della, they're very few. We don't have to get married right away. I ask that you just spend the night with me. Just let me hold you?"

Della had accepted that proposal and they stayed in a quaint bed and breakfast right near the park. They had downed two bottles of merlot while talking of goals, even children. The entire night was a blur, and they had barely touched. When Della woke up to the aroma of cinnamon pancakes, her new prize was still parked outside. She had not dreamed that one at all.

"Sweetheart, I want you to park the car in your garage until I get back into town. The insurance is still pending and I want it to have full coverage in case something happens." Della had not thought twice about the request. "Well, where are you going in the meantime?" she asked.

Edward had checked the time, threw on his uniform that had been pressed at the dry cleaners next door, and said he had a plane to catch. "This time I'll be back before you know it."

Two weeks, the usual timeframe, had passed. Edward had called from the airport and said he would be waiting on the curb outside the baggage claim. Again, the man had taken it for granted that Della could drop her caseload anytime she wanted, interrupt plans with family, and cut her responsibilities short whenever he beckoned. And she did.

Once he hopped into the passenger side, Della lashed out: "What happened to you, Edward? It's been two weeks and you haven't even called. I asked myself how I could be treated to such spectacular gifts, then be dropped like a hot potato whenever you see fit. Don't you believe in planning? How about informing me the next time you're going to see me, and perhaps we can make it happen mutually."

"You did not do anything wrong, Della. I'm a busy

man. I told you that the first time we got together. I was in New York City taking care of business."

"Business? What kind of business would prompt you to stay away without calling? At least you could have called to say hello. I feel like you've built me up and now that I want you, you're set to drop me."

"Della, I did not mean to leave you hanging. It's getting harder and harder for me to part from you. I think we should go home now and spend some quality time together. It's long overdue." Edward rolled his up his sleeves and threw his tie in the backseat. He then squeezed her thigh so hard, Della jumped. Before she could protest, Edward reached over and kissed her neck with his full, luscious lips.

"I know you had a life before you met me and may have been more interested in David at some time. I have held my desire for you inside my heart. I often think about what it would be like to make love to you. I dream about holding you and kissing your sweet lips at night, tasting your flavor and feeling your passion. I want you desperately. With my job, I can't be with you all the time. I know I should call you but if I don't, does that mean our relationship should collapse?"

Della had listened to every word Edward said as she drove cautiously down the road. The sky was dark and gloomy. There was a loud thunder and then it began to rain. "Edward, did you know it was going to rain today?"

"I had no idea. I'm glad it didn't rain during the flight. Of course, we just fly over it." The highway turned slippery and the rain crashed down harder. The windows began to fog up and Della could not see. Edward told her to turn on the defogger, but within seconds, they'd been rear-ended. Della pulled to the right shoulder and Edward got out of the car.

Only minutes later, Edward hopped back in the car as if nothing had happened. "Oh, it was a college student in Daddy's truck. There's no damage. Go on, Della."

"Edward, are you sure? This is a white car, I'm sure something is visible. Did you get his information? We could wait for the police." She was angry that Edward had been so nonchalant about a $50,000 car.

"Relax. There's no need for the police. The car has a pliable rubber bumper. That's exactly what he hit. Now let's get home so I can play with your body."

Della was enticed. She had waited weeks for him to talk to her like that. Besides, she hadn't slept with David in quite some time either.

Once they had settled into her place and Edward finally finished drilling Della about her antiques, they decided to order Thai food. Feeling "ravenous," Edward had called for four meals instead of two. "You know, baby, they usually give a lot of food. Who is going to eat four dinners? The Swimming Angel tofu is enough to feed five." Yes, he had acted strange that day, and the car thing was only the beginning.

Edward said he wanted enough food for two days because he planned on ravishing her for that amount of time. "Look, you must think I do not have a profession to tend to. Yes, I can work from home most of the time, but if I don't clock a certain amount of hours, my peers know it. We do have a very stable reputation as you're aware of."

For once, Edward Dawson was through with talking. He undressed in front of her and asked her to come upstairs with him. "Now? The food's going to be here within thirty minutes. I thought you were famished!" Della laughed and stood there dumbfounded. Edward only had his silk black briefs on now.

"I've got a lot of energy from sitting all day. What better way than to spend it on you. Don't you think we've waited long enough, Della?" This was definitely a different side of Edward. *Hello?* Hadn't she tried to make a move on him a dozen times before? Once, she even wore no bra on purpose so he could spot her nipples in a see-through blouse.

"Okay, let's eat first. I didn't even have breakfast

today. Then I'll shut the phone off and we'll have all night. We can even rent some sexy films if you'd like." Della couldn't believe how lackadaisical she had become around this man. He enjoyed it and kissed her lovingly on the lips.

After they ate, Edward did not want to stay home after talking about spending quality time. The night was still young and the holiday season was beginning and he wanted to be the first to see the Christmas lights after Thanksgiving. The open spirit of giving was in the air. He wanted to take Della to the nicest mall in town.

The next forty-eight hours were a whirlwind. Della did not have the courage to tell Neilmore about the $30,000 shopping spree Edward had enticed her to spring on herself! The mink coat at Saks, the matching sapphire ring, necklace and bracelet she bought after he said he would pay the bill the following week from his wire account. Had Della James gone insane? She charged all of it on her Visa. It had been the happiest shopping day of her life.

"I just can't imagine how my friends would feel if they knew I had a man like you," she told Edward in one of the stores.

"The world is *jealous*." he said matter-of-factly. "They can't have me. I'm yours,"

"Edward, being born rich isn't easy, is it?" Della

asked. "Do you worry about folks coming after your father's deeds?" While listening to her, he had finally opened up about his family's lifestyle.

"To tell you the truth, I think about it less than I talk about it, Della. His money has helped me find out who I am and where in the world I fit."

They were walking around the Underground, tooling in and out of stores, touching and trying on stuff to make each other laugh. They had acted like high schoolmates. Della in a mink midi coat. Edward with a band of pearls around his head. They fell comfortably in and out of conversation. She had believed that she finally broke through Edward's icy, one-dimensional exterior.

"How long does it take you to get tired of something you really thought you liked?" Edward asked.

"Like what?"

Edward pointed to a pair of diamond earrings and a matching necklace. "Like that set. if you really thought you loved it, how long would it take for you to be bored with it?"

"I don't know, Edward. I suppose we all feel like there's something better to buy when the urge strikes."

"How long will it take for you to get tired of me?" He asked. He pulled her into him, right in the middle of the promenade, held her face so he could look into her brown eyes, and then he kissed Della.

One kiss at first, just the slight warm touch of his olive lips to hers. When Della didn't resist, he moved back in. The same kiss, short and sweet, but harder than the first. He parted her lips with his own and slowly sucked the tip of her tongue in his mouth.

Della stepped back, still in his embrace and smiled. "I could get used to that."

Edward led her over to the food court where they sat and talked. He was on call. That's how his life was. Could she feel safe and secure with a man like him? She later told Edward.

"Edward, I trust you in spite of the bizarre things you've sprung on me without a moment's notice. You make me very happy and safe." They returned to her place with all the packages. Della was tingling all over.

CHAPTER *Thirteen*

Both of them were exhausted from dealing with the holiday crowds. "Edward, thank you for the gifts. I'll put them up tomorrow. From the look on your face I think you are ready for bed."

Within minutes there were splashes of rain on the window pane. There was a burst of thunder. Edward told Della, "This reminds me of a song, 'Oh What a Night' by a group called The Dells."

"I remember that song. As a matter of fact I have it. Do you want to hear it?"

"No, not now. I'll just fall asleep. Let's take our shower and go to sleep." Edward and Della undressed and got into the shower together. This was the first time she saw Edward nude. She was seriously stirred up. They began to kiss and touch one another as the warm water trickled down their excited skin. The radiance of passion was now a frozen moment in time and the world outside no longer existed. They wanted each other. Della was involved in the moment of passion and she wanted to feel the fantasy of relaxing in her bed of rose petals with sweet smelling candles burning in the room. She tenderly kissed Edward's lips and she held him as he grew stronger.

"Edward, let's save this sensation for the bedroom. Let's get out of the shower and dry off." She had walked to her dresser and opened a bottle of rose petals. Before Edward dried off, they were sprinkled all over the bed. Then she lit her candles and turned on some jazz. As Edward stretched out on the bed he looked out the window and watched the rain. He said, "Della, I feel so lucky to have you here." Then he asked her to lie on her stomach.

Edward stroked Della's hair and kissed the back of her neck. He gently caressed her back as he ran his tongue down the sides of her sweet smelling body. Edward used his tongue to tickle her hips and inner thighs as he moved gently down to her feet to massage her toes. He rubbed her feet as he slowly sucked her big toe. Then Della turned over. He lifted her right leg with her toes pointed to the ceiling. The intimacy of the position was startling as he used his mouth to take every inch of her in. She felt the pressure of his lips on her clitoris. She was familiar with the rush. He was slow, smooth and powerful as her juices flowed. Della could not move. Both legs were now in the air.

"No, no, I don't want to come like this. I want you in me!" she exclaimed. It was too late. She screamed, "Oh God!" She arched her back, struggling to adjust her position. Edward knew he was in charge. He smiled and laid his head on her stomach as he blew his warm wind between her thighs. When Della's body began to relax and her tension was gone, Edward moved to her lips. He shrugged his wide brown shoulders as she hooked her hand around his head. "Della, you feel so good," he moaned. Then he rubbed his smoothly shaved cheek against her turgid nipple and took the stiff morsel in his mouth.

Now Della knew this was the prelude to the symphony of affection as she felt the blunt head of his sex nudging against her stomach. Della was ready and he expressed his manhood as he slid strongly into her. She arched her back while struggling to feel the fullness of his pleasure. Edward was not in a rush as he held himself. The tension began to build again as she rocked against him, deeper and deeper. The moment had come when he could no longer contain himself. He took a quick breath and collapsed. Both of them expressed the deep, guttural sounds of completion. It had continued to rain the rest of the night and Della slept in Edward's arms until the late morning hours.

CHAPTER Fourteen

The following evening, Edward appeared at the door. Della was beside herself with emotion from the night before. Waves of sex and flower scents still mingled in her bedroom. "What's wrong, Edward?"

"I've got a serious situation, Della. I don't know if you've been watching the news, but all hell is breaking loose."

"What news and what hell?"

"It's my father. Seems like some of his enemies have caught on to him hiding out and they've seized all his assets."

"Is he okay?"

"I'm not sure, but my life is going to be a wreck. I just don't know what to do." Was she seriously talking to the man who had taken charge of her body hours before? They only parted because Edward had to go to a convention in the area. Of course Della had not been watching the news. She had been desperately trying to focus on work for the last six hours.

"Take off your coat, Edward. Calm down and I'll make us a drink."

She came back in a flash with two champagne spritzers. Nothing to celebrate except for the fact that Della finally had sex with Edward Dawson. That was sure something.

"This is so unlike me to be caught out of pocket like this. Every liquid penny in the world I had access to… "

"Is what? Edward, talk to me."

"Tied up with my father's. Those assets are frozen. Frozen! I just found out."

"How much do you need?" Della asked. "I mean, you still have your property and all that, so you can't be completely out of pocket. Can you?"

"No, Della. I mean, I don't know. I'm so confused." Edward stood up, then sat back down abruptly. He wrung his hands and dropped his head in disappointment.

"What kind of man could ask his lady friend for a loan? Della, do you think I am the kind of man who can't take care of my business? Believe me, I couldn't stand that. What am I going to do?" There is a deal I could make immediately to jumpstart his cash flow if I had your help. I feel for him. This had never happened to him before. It was foul just how it was happening now.

"Things happen, Edward. It's not your fault." Della felt overwhelming compassion for him. She wondered if she was falling in love with him or if her feelings were simply heightened from the night before. Della assured him she would get a cash advance the following day during bank hours.

"Della, I'm a good man."

"I know that, Edward." She knew he was a good man, she believed it in her heart. He couldn't need that much money, could he?

It had been $20,000, nearly all of Della's savings. She paused before initiating the withdrawal, but eventually approved it. Della James had trusted a man enough to let him swindle years of savings from her *and* charge up her own credit card on herself. But that wasn't even enough. After receiving the money, Edward had begged Della to sign for a small loan to make up for the rest of the money he needed. In a stupor, she had obliged. He was leaving on an afternoon flight, and said he would call her when he arrived at his destination.

That day, Della drove Edward to the airport. He tearfully told her that she didn't have to stay and wait for him to board. He requested time alone in the President Circle's Lounge before getting on the plane. The lounge was reserved for travel executives.

"Della, I've never said it but I think you already know that I love you," Edward had said while getting his bags out of the backseat. "I really do." She believed him with all her heart.

"I wish you could walk to the President Circle's Club and show off that new mink coat, but I can take it from here." He signaled he would call and puckered his juicy lips into a kiss.

"By the way, who won that land fill case?" Edward had known the case was another victory for Della, but he wanted to show interest in her.

"The litigation was settled and our law firm representing the plaintiff prevailed."

"Thanks," Edward beamed. "That information is money in the bank, sweetheart."

Della never saw Edward again. All this time, she had kept so much to herself. Della knew she'd been a fool and it was too much to admit to another soul.

CHAPTER *Fifteen*

WINTER 2001

Neilmore rolled up in front of the Goldberg build-ing just as Goldberg and Wanda were returning from lunch. She knew the coast was clear of Della for a little while because she told Neilmore she would be in meetings all day, only stopping to take in lunch. After Neilmore had listened to the *entire* Ed-ward Dawson saga, Neilmore was compelled to take action. She tooted her horn and called out Wanda's name from the driver's seat.

"Hey Neilmore, what's up?"

"Got a minute, Wanda? Please get in." Self-as-sured and poised, Wanda slid into the passenger side. Neilmore handed Wanda her card. "Wait, give it back. You'll need my cell phone and direct line too."

"What's up, Neilmore, you looking for work?"

"Not at this time, but I do need your help. An odd request but I'm confident you'll agree to it. I need you to keep me informed the minute you hear anything, see anything out of the ordinary that has to do with Della James."

Wanda puckered her lips like a fish. "Okay... would you like to give me something to go on? Aren't you supposed to be the right-hand pal of the illustrious Della James?"

"I can't tell you anything else. I know you hate Della, but this is in the firm's best interest too."

"Hate is a strong verb, Neilmore. There are milder and socially correct terms to describe our mutual dislike. Why on earth would I want to help Della, if that's what is being implied here?" Wanda opened Neilmore's car door to scoot out.

Neilmore grabbed her shoulder and pinned it back to the seat.

"Let me see. Your face, Goldberg's married face plastered all over Atlanta news. No, make that national news. I have acquaintances at CNN. Is that a good enough reason or do you need the video version?"

"I have your card," Wanda huffed before sliding out of the car.

"Oh, Wanda, you can keep sleeping with Goldberg. We wouldn't want to stop your pleasure there. But let this be a reminder to you: pick your enemies more careful and take less pleasure in the future in making a fellow co-worker's life miserable."

Wanda slammed the door and strutted into her office, late from lunch again.

Neilmore drove off, back to her own world of law. Della had told her about her days at Goldberg before she went *of counsel*. That time as an in-house attorney at Goldberg surely took the case for rat race. Della said she couldn't trust Wanda further than she could spit. Wanda would do anything to get ahead.

Meantime, Wanda was shaken by Neilmore's odd request and she was determined to get to the bottom of it. She wanted to confront Della in her office. As she approached, Wanda saw the door open and she could hear Della chastising a new attorney.

"You can't always be a quick start. You have to study your cases properly, prepare your oral argument thoroughly so you won't look like a fool in front of the judge and jury. It is imperative that you follow the judge's procedures and schedules. I wrote everything down for you before you go in front of Judge Walsh. He can be a real prick, but stay tough." The new attorney laughed. Wanda smiled in spite of herself. For nearly an hour, Della coached the other woman on scheduled court proceedings and motion status, trial preparation and verdict forms. Wanda was impressed.

"So Jennifer, if you have any questions, please do not hesitate to call me anytime. Here's my home number since I do most of my preliminary work there." Wanda crept back to her office before they could see her. Minutes passed and neither of them left Della's office.

Wanda figured that Della was getting in good with the new girl on the block. Wanda was not threatened at all. She had already commanded the entire firm of gentlemen to bow down, and most of the press called her for insight on the firm's cases.

CHAPTER *Sixteen*

Jamie had been making the drive into Joan's antique shops and Terrence's real estate offices to manage their books since she was seventeen. She had been driving in so long she could almost do it blindfolded.

When Della was thirteen, *going on twenty-one* as Jamie saw it, and declared at the dinner table that she was going to be an attorney, Jamie was seventeen really trying to just be seventeen. She fancied herself the more sensible one of the two.

Jamie could hear them now. Her mother would say, "Della is so smart. She *already* knows she is going to be someone important some day. She reminds me of my mother. You know, Jamie, Sophonie was a very determined woman. She wanted things done her way. Even when Sophonie was wrong, she was still indisputably right in some way. Della is just like my mother–determined! You know, it takes determination and discipline to make it in this world. You can't make a hot buttered biscuit without determination and discipline." The spiel sounded like a broken record.

Terrence would follow suit. Jamie could see them around the dinner table and hear her daddy say, "Joan, Ebenezer Baptist was dynamite this morning, wasn't it, girls? Rev gave a good sermon, talked about discrimination partially and nepotism everywhere, even in the home. My kids may have to face it in the world but they'll never have to at home," and wouldn't he head straight for the couch right after dinner to catch the sports shows. He would yell, "Della, you comin'?"

When her parents started grooming her, insisting she help out with their businesses, Jamie didn't mind. She'd do whatever it took to be important to Mama and Daddy.

Besides, Della is a fool. Why work so hard? Mama and Daddy have more money than the law allows.

Sometimes Jamie would summon a road buddy to make the ride more interesting, offer to drive one of her parent's employees just for companionship. But that got stale quick. Either they'd run their mouths way too much about all their own personal business or they would sleep all the way in. Jamie sure wasn't into disclosing any of her business and who needs a snoozer for a road buddy? However, since Jamie didn't mind putting *Della's* business in the street, she would entertain the carpooling every now and then.

Otherwise, *thank the lord for speaker phones*, she'd just talk to herself on the long ride in and look just like all the folks she saw yakking away in their cars, seeming like they were talking to themselves.

One day while driving to the fabric store to pick up products for her mother, Jamie realized that she had forgotten Joan's checkbook back at the house. It was nearly forty-five minutes away, but she had to turn back because she never carried cash. Despite the incidental fender benders on the highway, Jamie made it back to the house in record time.

And what had she found beside Mama's checkbook?

Della making out on the couch with the light-skinned boy Jammie liked, Carl Wynan. It was a sight to see. Della's copper lipstick caked all over his smooth baby face, her bra strap down past her elbow. Jamie had called Della a slut. Della didn't blink an eye. She spat out that Carl did not belong to anyone, as Jamie had not officially claimed him. Della hadn't counted all the phone calls they made to each other nor the fact that Jamie wasn't interested in anyone else at the time. That day laid the foundation for the real sister rivalry to come.

When Jamie should have been a senior in college, she was a freshman. She had taken the time to work her parents' businesses before finally deciding to study Architecture at the Georgia Institute of Technology. She could have gone anywhere in the world but she chose the school because of her parents. They were so family oriented, Jamie did not want to break her mother's heart like Della had by gallivanting from city to city.

Once when Neilmore was trying to heal the distance between Della and Jamie, she asked Jamie point blank, "Y'all don't get along, huh? Why is that?"

By the time Neilmore asked she had been around the James' home for years and Jamie was comfortable answering, "Not really, Neilmore. It's been that way a long time, too."

Neilmore, full of other James family stories, was careful not to pick too deeply with Jamie. Neilmore remembered how Terrence and sometimes Joan enthusiastically referred to Della's birth year as the year, "Praise Jesus, we Atlantans got our first Black mayor, Jackson Maynard, the Black millionaire maker," and if she asked about Jamie's year of birth, it would be just a number.

Neilmore gathered that's what it must have been like for Jamie to have been the only child for four years. Then Della appeared and stole every bit of her possible light, every minute of the day.

Even Jamie could admit Della was born a go-getter but she couldn't forgive her for all the mental beatings that had stacked up during the course of their adulthood. As Jamie dutifully tried to earn her mother and father's attention by handling family business responsibly and by being a considerate older sister (at least in their eyes), Della would always steal the limelight. Della this, Della that. Della sent a letter on a napkin from New York and a painting of herself done by a famous artist. Della's in Amsterdam, Brazil, Guinea, Nigeria, Kenya, South Africa, Paris, Japan. Della, Della, Della.

Jamie was sick of it, and from what she had confided in Neilmore, had been for the longest.

Jamie told Neilmore, "I waited and waited for Della to grow up and at least once give me my props for being. I thought even if Mama and Daddy can't, Della can and will. But she never did, Neilmore, and I got tired of waiting." And when Jamie laughed out of control like a time bomb with a faulty timer about to blow, Neilmore quickly changed the subject.

Unlike Della, Jamie was hard to clock. One thing was certain and maybe it was a family trait Neilmore picked up on, but they were all stubborn as hell and if Jamie said she was tired of waiting, she meant it… period. And the way Neilmore saw it, the whole Marlon episode had formed a blister in Jamie's mind that continued to fester.

Jamie had met Marlon through Della but when she ran into him again at school, he seemed like another person completely. He was the star of the basketball team, disciplined and artistic. He fantasized about ditching sports for law school and he eventually did. She had guessed that Della's world of law made a lasting impression on everyone she screwed.

They made their first date over a biscotti and cheap coffee from the cart that was wheeled around campus every morning. Her studies were tough and the program was very competitive, rated among the top ten in the country. She probably wasn't friendly to anyone that year, but Marlon confessed his attraction to her after Della left for Harvard. Marlon once told Jamie during their early courtship these words.

"Jamie, I saw you when I had Della on my arm and my initial thought was that perhaps I could have you both." She had snickered. "But then I decided that the older one should always win the trophy."

"Oh, why is that?" Jamie had taken time out from studying the designs of William Douglas Caroë, her favorite modern architect. Her brain was completely fried after reading all night.

They both laughed. Jamie liked his personality right away and wondered who he was seeing. She did not mention Della's name. Her parents had still been torn up about her leaving town.

"I have to run to practice, but I'd like to take you out tonight. Do you have to study?" At least he'd been respectful of school, unlike so many other ball players in Atlanta, the strip club capitol of the nation.

"Don't you have a game tonight?"

"Yes, but we're going to win and I want you to celebrate with me." Jamie said yes. She was flattered and hooked from that day on.

Marlon's team had won that night and he didn't even wait around to talk to the other guys. He was parked in the back parking lot, where it began to rain. They decided to go to Fat Matt's Rib Shack, a greasy Southern and blues spot in town. As Marlon drove on the interstate, the sky turned pitch black and other cars pulled over under the bypass. "Jamie, I've got to stop the car because I don't feel safe driving. If you're real hungry, there are some Oreos in the glove compartment." Jamie didn't care about food. She was just fine alone with him in the tight front seat of his Jetta.

"Don't worry, I promise not to try anything," Marlon remarked. Jamie's curiosity was peaked, considering her sister had probably screwed him a thousand times knowing her. However, Marlon kept his word and only read some poetry he'd written.

"I wrote this poem called 'In Search Of'. Would you like to hear it?" Jamie never said no to a helpless romantic, and she could already tell that Marlon was one. It was refreshing.

A woman walking across the street with red shoes and a short red skirt is in search of, Men in suits standing against the wall with alcohol drinks in their hand in search of,

Wanting to buy a car to make you look a certain way, because you are in search of,

You go here, you go there, to find a better opportunity because you are in search of a better life, You listen and don't talk to hear a better way in search of more opportunity; In search of the moments you missed by not taking your responsibility; In search of another chance to be a man with someone else's children; In search of a reason you justify your poor judgment, or lack thereof, In search of a thrill, in search of a spare, in search of pocket change, in search of commitment, In search of acceptance, in search of family, in search of a man, in search of a woman, In search of that touch to make you feel a special way, In search of a drug to help you hide from things you cannot stand to face

As we grow tired we are in search of ourselves, in search of our lives to be what the search tells us We MUST be in search of.

Marlon carefully folded the piece of paper and waited for Jamie's response. She didn't say anything. "So, what do you think?"

"It was nice for a beginner."

"What beginner? I'm past the beginner writing stage. My poetry sets the course of my bond or understanding with anybody. My work is so personal, someone has to be committed to my work to be committed to me."

"Wow, you're the same guy that was on that court tonight?" Jamie wondered if Della liked Marlon's impassioned writing. She found him to be pretty emotional too.

"Do you know how many women come around me just to associate with my success? I'm not just about basketball or working out, I have intellect and other goals besides being the star. Do you feel me?" The water pounded on the roof. Jamie wondered how long they'd be stuck like this. She nodded her head for him to continue.

"I know sports dominate our society as an escape and an economic force. I know that athletes become movie stars, but I'm more interested in politics and government. I believe in the human spirit. I think every generation wants to improve itself. Each human spirit will quietly design its own destiny by working out its own fate to a more productive future. We are all destined to do that."

Marlon would follow his dreams better than anyone else. He wanted his poetry to transform the globe and his basketball to fund literacy. He wanted to change the face of poverty, violence and homelessness. During Jamie's marriage to him, she couldn't count the number of advocacy groups Marlon had wrapped himself around.

While sports agents had offered Marlon huge sums of money to sign onto a team, he was apprehensive. On the other hand, when Habitat for Humanity said they wanted to photograph Marlon while helping to build a house for a needy family, the man was elated. The photographs came with a lengthy story on Marlon's contributions to urban Atlanta.

And yet, Jamie could not be inspired by Marlon.

CHAPTER *Seventeen*

Jamie wrapped her hair up before sliding into the lavender bubbles. After seeing how haggard Della looked, she had some hardcore thinking to do. They flailed around in a web of love and hate for sure, but Jamie did not wish so much misery on anyone. Perhaps Marlon had influenced her more than she wanted to admit during their ten years of marriage. He possessed a large heart and a pure desire to do the right thing ninety-nine percent of the time. Jamie knew she was a very lucky woman to have him.

As she lowered her body into the warm water, Jamie closed her eyes with determination. These moments were the only ones that brought full meditation for her since her brain was always so busy calculating numbers or executing design plans. The emotions–the hate and the emptiness–had a constant presence too. Why had Jamie never felt truly happy? The question nagged on a daily basis. Sure, there were happy times but she wasn't sure if she had ever experienced a true state of contentment, in spite of her blessings.

While in the tub, Jamie set her wedding ring on the floor. The one with emerald inlays that Marlon's grandmother passed on to her. It was one of the most elegant pieces of jewelry she had ever laid eyes on. It still bothered Jamie to think that Della could have been the one wearing it. Those days, Jamie was paranoid her sister would entice Marlon to come back to her any minute before they exchanged vows. The thought almost destroyed Jamie.

Later that evening Jamie got dressed and went to visit her mother. While sitting in the kitchen with her mother the mood was very relax.

"Now don't let me have to pull it out of you, Jamie. What do you want your daddy and I to give y'all for renewing your wedding vows?" Joan had asked, pulling something down from over the stove days before the ceremony.

It was the first time in a long time they were alone to really talk as mother and daughter. The house had been like a busy railroad station, planners coming in, seamstresses leaving, rehearsal folks colliding, the baker, the florist, photographer, church folks, excited neighbors.

"Mama, I already feel so special. I mean having the chance to renew our wedding vows here, what more could I ask you and Daddy for?"

"Whatever contents your heart. And I mean that."

Jamie cried. "Mama, do you and Daddy love me as much as you love Della?"

Joan turned around, surprised to see the tears flowing down Jamie's face. She ran water over a clean towel and came to press it to Jamie's face. "Jamie, you have a case of the jitters. Girl, what kind of question is that?"

Her mother held her and rocked her a minute. Jamie wiped her tears, saying she felt like such a fool. "You got the jitters, baby. That's all. Everyone gets them. I know you are more sure of yourself than that. We love you both equally for who you are. Where Della is bold, you're quiet. Where she's aggressive, you're discreet. That's always been okay, Jamie. Your father and I are so pleased with you, Jamie." Her mother rocked her like a child.

"You're a good daughter, Jamie. The best. The way you stayed with us and helped manage both of our businesses instead of going straight to college. Honey, we still haven't found anyone like you when it comes to accounting; in fact, your expertise has helped us sleep so much easier." Her mother stroked the side of her face gently.

"And you know we love Marlon. He's family too. He's like the son Daddy never had. So smart, so kind, reliable and eager to do something important around here as an attorney. Jamie, we are so pleased with you. We really are. Does that rest your heart?" Joan waited for Jamie to smile. She didn't that day. She had just wanted their love, and you couldn't wrap that up in a wedding gift.

Months later, Joan and Terrence had surprised Jamie and Marlon with a new house, complete with a woodworking studio and library.

"Did you see my big girl's studio? I knew Jamie would be crazy about the way we laid out her architecture studio, I just knew it!" her father exclaimed to Marlon. Jamie had listened to the conversation from the staircase.

"She is so pleased, and my library and office aren't shabby either, Dad. We will be eternally grateful."

"You are most welcome, son. Now you listen to me, I don't interfere in my children's personal lives, never have and never will. But I have to know this. Do you love your wife?"

"I do with all my heart," Marlon had replied with such sincerity. "You know, Dad, as quiet as it's kept,

TOO GOOD TO BE USED ▪ 153

I am so lucky Della was not deeply interested in me. Della and I could never have shared the true, deep love Jamie and I have for each other."

"Dad, you're a man of your word and I'll take that promise of yours to heart. I have one for you too. You never have to worry about your daughter with me. As long as she'll have me, I'll be here."

And as Jamie looked back now, hadn't Marlon been right in her corner? Encouraging her, guiding her, trying to be her strength until she found her own?

Jamie remembered looking back over the patio into the backyard. It was summer. *Like the day she had stayed in her room all afternoon making a Father's Day card. She had cut and pasted, colored and written, made her poem so pretty she couldn't wait the days until Father's Day to give her daddy his special card. She was about eight years old. She ran down the big stairs so fast and out the side door. The sun was shining, the flowers were bouncing, it smelled so fresh and so sweet. She skipped, singing, "Daddy, Daddy" to herself. He was probably in the garage working on some of Mama's antiques. Jamie looked but he was not there.*

She skipped on to the backyard and there he was, pushing Della on the white swing he built for her on the big oak tree. They were laughing. "Daddy, Daddy!" Jamie could not contain her happiness and called out. She kept wiping

her hands on her dress to make sure not to ruin his card.
Her father opened his arms as she ran to him and when she
was almost there, Della fell out of the swing. Mama heard
Della scream and came running out of the house to pick
Della up. Daddy followed Mama and Della in. And there
Jamie stood with her card, the empty swing still flying in
the afternoon of a spoiled surprise.

Jamie contemplated seeing a therapist for her anger, depression and anxiety but she did not do it.

CHAPTER *Eighteen*

After slumming on the couch for three days and entertaining Neilmore with endless stories about Edward, Della was fully prepared to return to the office. She got back into her usual routine of yoga and an oatmeal-honey facial before reviewing the present caseload in her study. She even thought about finishing the green painting, but decided to wait until the evening. If the whole world knew that Edward Dawson had really misused her, then so be it. Della James would regain her pride in no time.

Della shadowed the new attorney most of the morning and was in high spirits throughout lunch. She was so thrilled to connect with another female at the firm, she had even invited Jennifer to dinner that evening. Then the unthinkable happened. The telephone rang and the receiver lit up Jeremy Goldberg's extension.

"Hi Della, I need to see you in my office as soon as possible."

"Sure, Mr. Goldberg. How was your weekend?" He did not answer but hung up the phone swiftly. Della took a deep breath and took her time walking the length of the hall to his door, which was open. It's incredible how fast the mind can imagine a dozen scenarios while in the panic zone. Had the press misspelled the firm's name wrong in the land fill case? Was she in trouble for wearing a short skirt today? Would she be reprimanded for using the company phone to make international calls?

"Della, close the door behind you and take a seat please," Goldberg said, taking his wire rim glasses off and rubbing his eyes. His face was flushed.

"Della, you do awesome work for the firm and you have helped us establish our reputation in this city and nationally. All the partners are happy with you."

Oh, Wanda too? she thought. Goldberg's eyes changed and began to sink deep into his face. He looked away as he spoke. "Della, we got the report that you have been in some kind of trouble with the police. This does not look good for the firm. You know how the press is; they embellish anything worth tearing their claws into. I'm going to have to suspend you until the matter is resolved."

Della was speechless. Minutes before, she was teaching someone else how to command the world of law. She cleared her throat. "Well, sounds like you know more about my situation than I do. I'm still trying to figure it out. Mr. Goldberg, you know I am not a criminal, for God's sake, I've never even had a speeding ticket..."

He cut her off before she could ramble on in a nervous state. "We got an image to maintain, Della. We can't keep anyone around who may have a problem with moral turpitude. We all have personal lives, but some things get out very quickly."

"So how did you find out that I was arrested?" Della stared down at her lush red nails that she'd painted herself for once. She did it in celebration of feeling good this morning.

"News travels very fast from trusted sources. I got to make this short and sweet. Della, clear your office and pack up your things before everyone else gets back from court. I'll call you later in the week to get a report on the status of cases you're assigned to, then pass everything to Jennifer and Wanda." That magic name again. Della had a fleeting thought that Wanda had somehow found out about the trouble, but it didn't make any sense.

She dropped her head remorsefully and left his office. As Della charged into her office, Wanda stood near the drinking fountain, stone-faced. Della packed her things in a flash and sped home in tears.

CHAPTER *Nineteen*

A MONTH LATER

Della was living on her thirst for revenge on the elusive Edward Dawson, and living on every kind of ice cream ever created. Like Jamie, she stuffed herself like a hog whenever there was a crisis. At least they had shared that in common since childhood.

After returning from the grocery store a month after she exited Goldberg, there was a certified letter in the front door. It was from the State Bar Association. She dropped her bags and rushed inside to the kitchen table to open it. The letter was to inform her that she was scheduled for a hearing regarding charges of moral turpitude. If never ever before, Della finally knew the meaning of demise. It stared her in the face, shattering every case she had worked on, every case that brought a victory. She was nearly breathless.

As if on cue, the phone rang. "Leave me alone!" Della shouted to thin air.

Her tears came in a rage. Meantime, whoever was on the other line had not given up after a dozen rings. Della picked it up furiously. "What?"

"Hello, Della, this is Edward."

Della was at a loss for words. She hung up the telephone. The phone rang again immediately. After the tenth ring, she picked it up.

"Della, are you there? Please do not hang up the phone. I must see you."

She gained her composure and held him on the line while contacting Marlon's office on her cell phone. Marlon instructed her to make a date with him. They were to meet at her house on Saturday morning. Edward begged to come over sooner, but Della insisted that she would be better prepared to talk in length with him over the weekend.

That Saturday morning at 8:00 a.m. Edward stood at Della's door in a navy blue suit, carrying a brief case. Della answered without using her intercom. The first thing out of Edward's quivering mouth was, "I love you."

"What?" she gasped. Della couldn't believe this

insincere monster masquerading as a human said the words so loosely.

"I know what I've done to you. I'm not bad at all. Please forgive me for what I've done. I've paid a price. The short time with you has turned my life around. I know now that love is not measured in moments of time, but in timeless moments. I asked God to forgive me and now I ask you, Della."

He promised to repay the loan, marry her, buy "another" car, whatever it took to be with her again. Della invited him into the living room while she excused herself to make coffee. She calmly called the police who were waiting around the corner. Della took a deep breath and mumbled a prayer before going back to the living room.

Edward must have been suspicious because he was gone when Della returned.

CHAPTER *Twenty*

....

"Wanda, I don't know if I should be talking to you right now. What, are you inviting me to a party to celebrate my downfall?"

"Look, I know you and me are not on the best of terms. As a matter of fact, we're barely on any terms at all, huh? But I don't want to see this happen to you. I'm not your friend, but in spite of recent surveys, I'm not your enemy, either. Please understand." Della did not have any words for this woman.

The shocking call came twenty-four hours after she let Edward escape. She begged Marlon to slap her silly once he arrived with a whole swat team to find no one but her crumbled on the couch. Speechless, Marlon just retrieved a few sleeping pills from her medicine cabinet and handed them to her with a glass of water before calmly locking the door behind him.

"Okay, guessing game's over, Wanda. Why the hell are you calling me? I'm not feeling particularly friendly right now anyway."

"Rightly so, Della. But there are people in your life that care about you and this may be a shocker to you… I'm one of them."

"Oh, how did I deserve this lucky day?" Della did not control her tears.

"Della, I'm going to help you get through this and keep your license. Please meet me as soon as possible."

"Wanda, this is all hitting me so fast, I don't know what to say…"

"Della, I want you to come over to my house where we'll have some privacy.

"Be there at 6:00 tonight and I'll leave work early. I'm in the Mayfair, the second floor loft. Will I see you then?"

Della did a quick assessment of her situation before responding. Who did she have at this point to represent her? Who could she even afford? Neilmore would be too emotional. She could see her in front of a judge now. Della sighed and agreed to meet Wanda.

The day went by fast. Della stayed in a mindless state waiting for the appointment to come. Edward had invaded her thoughts. Sneering and eating cake.

Singing to her in a ballroom and dancing with her in the kitchen. Penetrating her, then begging for money the next day. The images made her feel dead. He was not a real man and the events were nothing but one long dream.

"Della, I'm glad to see you. You're right on time, but then again, you've always been very punctual." Wanda stood at the door in jeans and a tank top. Her long blonde hair was pulled into a twist. Della had never seen her in anything but suits that oozed with top salary dollars. She could not believe she was standing on Wanda Durham's porch.

Wanda nudged her in the door quickly. She took Della's jacket and handed her a sifter of brandy before leading her downstairs to the den. "Della, sit down and relax. I'm not going to hurt you." Wanda took a seat at her massive cherry wood desk and looked long and hard at Della.

Della surveyed the pictures on the walls. All live action shots of the woman she thought despised her since day one at the firm. Wanda was quite an athlete. She raced cars, climbed mountains, played soccer, and went deep sea fishing. Della was curious about the Black woman on Wanda's arm in every other picture, but she wasn't there to discuss her personal life. Nonetheless, she didn't notice one man in the photographs—perhaps strange for a woman who had a reputation of being a man-eater.

"Della, you're in more trouble than you realize, I'm afraid," Wanda finally spoke.

"Well maybe you know more than I do. Honestly, Wanda, what the hell is happening to me?"

"Della, I only know what's been communicated by the authorities. They've been swarming around like bees asking for your files and any details related to your personal life. I persuaded one of the detectives to give me the rundown. He was eyeing my legs the whole time, so I knew I could get something out of the bastard. I promised him a drink but never said when." Taking a sip of brandy, Wanda seemed proud of herself. Della could empathize. Maybe they weren't so different after all.

"We have to prepare your defense to go before the bar hearing and possible criminal prosecution right away, Della."

"Criminal, why criminal?"

"You received stolen property, didn't you? You're the only one that's been seen driving the car."

"Wanda, that is so lame! Anyone who knows me knows that I could have bought the car myself. My parents are substantially well-off, too. This is crazy."

"I know, but they will charge you. The asshole

conman is nowhere to be found and they've got to make use of tax dollars. You know the drill."

"Wanda, I don't believe this is happening to me." And with that, Della let her tears run vulnerably in front of someone whose intentions were still not known. She was glad to be in the company of another woman. Della had shut out Neilmore and Jamie practically since she'd been dismissed from the firm.

Wanda rushed to comfort Della, startling her with a hand on her back. "I just don't know what I'm going to do. I worked so hard all my life to get through school and elevate my career. All of it is in jeopardy because of my poor judgment of someone who should have never had that kind of power over me."

"Della, our emotions can wreak havoc when we're not expecting it. Did you love this man?" Both women straightened up in their seats and took another sip.

Della thought about the question.

"I guess almost… or at least enough to be played so viciously. Hell, I don't know. I did love his energy, his romance, his words, his body. As far as him, I don't even know who *he* was!"

"Della, no one deserves this type of pain. You're not alone. Now I want you to get a hold of yourself

and start from the beginning. I need to know everything that happened. How did you meet him?"

Della dreaded hashing all the details out again.
But with a swig of the brandy, she started from the
beginning, hoping Wanda would pick up on the per-
tinent facts and not the details that screamed Della
James was an idiot.

"I met him at the airport after getting back from
that weekend meeting on the Hawaii case. He was
dressed in a blue pilot's uniform and I thought he
was very handsome. We met for coffee the next
day. Or I should say he picked me up the next day
in a rented Lincoln Towncar." Della laughed at the
thought of it, the showy arrival for their first "date."

"So you thought he was a pilot?"

"Well, Wanda, I had no reason to believe he
wasn't."

"Who else knows about your relationship with
this man?"

"My friend Neilmore, who you met at the holiday
party last year, and my sister Jamie."

"Yes, I remember Neilmore but I don't think I've
met your sister before. How old is she? Are you
close?"

"Jamie is four years older than me. Are we close?
Close enough to see each other on a weekly basis,
I guess, but we've never been what you'd call the

ideal symbol of love to each other. There's years of hard feelings between us."

Wanda listened closely. It was strange for her to have Della James in her house as well, but she wasn't taking any chances. Wanda believed Neilmore's threats, so she figured she'd take matters into her own hands once the authorities stopped by the firm. In truth, she had not slept with Goldberg even though it appeared that way. She had done a very good job of concealing her own love life and for the sake of her partner, also a high profile attorney, she would keep it that way.

Besides, Wanda climaxed over a good challenge and she knew she could help Della with her eyes closed. The plea was easy: Love victimization.

"So where did the trouble come in, Della?"

Where should she begin, Della wondered. "The trouble started when I agreed to go to the car lot with him. The next incident was the shopping spree."

"Let me stop you there. What did he buy you?"

"Well, that's another screwed up problem. It's what I bought on my own credit cards."

"Della, how did that happen? I know us girls love to shop but..."

"We were in a rush and he did not have his checkbook. He asked me to charge everything until he got paid. A mink coat, set of jewelry, he made me spoil myself that day like an idiot!" Wanda stared at Della in disbelief.

"Look, everything you bought goes back. We are going to have to show the court you were a victim."

"Sounds easy, but that's not all. I also withdrew $20,000 from my savings account and signed for a loan, Wanda."

In the practice of law, Wanda Durham had heard it all, but she was completely floored that such a beautiful, intelligent woman could seriously get herself so conned. She figured the man had the charm of death or something. Seeing how distraught Della already was, Wanda kept her opinions to herself.

"We can use that documentation to further prove you were a victim of love.

Everybody falls for something or somebody they want until that very object turns on them. I'm so sorry, Della, but the real issue is now the vehicle. Naturally you did not know the car was stolen. Did you go with him to get it?"

"Yes, but I mostly stayed in the car and watched from a distance."

"You are still considered an accomplice. We just have to prove that you did not accept stolen property willingly so you won't be held for moral turpitude."

Della had stayed at Wanda's past midnight. They

devoured a pizza while Della told her everything she could remember about Edward. Wanda said she would forgo a retainer fee as long as they could put the past behind them. She also asked for full reign of the A-list cases for the next year if she got Della off the hook. It was a deal.

CHAPTER Twenty-one

Della was thoroughly depressed. She was relieved to have Wanda on her side in spite of their differences. The woman certainly knew how to fight a case, as Della had watched her oftentimes on the closed circuit monitor at the firm. This wasn't a practice battle. She hoped that Edward Dawson would be in the same room with her again just once. Della longed to release spitfire words and stare through him until his skin caught fire. Her whole life had been turned upside down and he was the smiling source.

The next day Della decided to take a book to her favorite coffeehouse and pass the hours buried in the glamorous lives of Sandra Brown's characters. Before she could sit down, an old acquaintance called her name from the other side of the room. Carol Dobbs, famous for all the gossip in law school. "Della, where have you been? Must be nice to see your name in the paper every other week!"

Della grimaced. "Girl, you've been settling cases left and right." Della was relieved to see someone from the past, who was connected to her before the Edward days. She welcomed any distraction.

Carol started in right away. "Della, remember Marsha? Tall, light-skinned girl in our class. She always knew everything before the professor even said it? Guess what, girlfriend, she was had!"

"Carol, some things never change. What happened?" Della ordered a latte and turkey sandwich before settling in for the tale.

Carol said, "Let me tell you. Last week she flew to Lagos, Nigeria for a convention. I got this information from her mother who told my mother what happened. When she arrived in Lagos she had to go through Customs. While going to Customs, the officer asked her if she were in the country for the World Convention of Female Attorneys. Marsha said yes. The agent was a well-groomed, middle-aged Black female who was wearing formal attire. She then asked her what hotel she could find her at. Marsha told her that she was staying at the Hilton. Then 'Lulu' said, 'That's nice, do you have anybody in town?' Marsha commented that she wasn't staying with anyone. They made plans to get together for a drink that evening. Marsha went through Customs and took a taxi to her hotel. The hotel was like a spacious kingdom with enormous ceiling fans, marble floors and wicker furniture. It was a beautiful place."

Della shook her head in amusement, patiently waiting for Carol to get to the real details. She had been the type to dominate any conversation, any dinner party with her irresistible, long tales.

"About three hours later, Lulu showed up in club gear. She had a bottle of white wine in her hand. Marsha didn't normally drink, but she took a glass out of politeness. Lulu asked her if she'd showered yet because she wanted to show her around town. Della, can you believe Marsha actually did get in that shower and left that strange woman alone with all her things? Then they turned on some music. Within thirty minutes, Marsha began to feel faint and she passed out!"

"Oh my god, that is so wrong!" Della blurted out. By this time, she had a mouthful of sandwich.

"Well, that's not the worst of it. When she woke up, all her clothes and things were gone. Vanished! She noticed the telephone line was cut. Marsha was completely out of it and she had no idea what to do. She cracked the door in hopes of seeing an attendant. She waited for hours in that state, Della! Finally she just left the room wrapped in the bed sheet. She went straight to the front desk in a stupor and told them that she had been robbed. The man at the counter just gazed at her body like an idiot, pretending he had not heard a word of what she screamed. Another attendant came from behind the desk and promised to call the police. She gave Marsha a bathrobe and soothed her until an officer came. He asked Marsha if she knew the woman and she told him that she had met her at Customs. The officer called the agency and no one had heard of a 'Lulu'."

Della shook her head in disgust, reflecting on her own situation. "Carol, there are people in this world that are just plain rotten, huh?"

"Well, get this – no one wanted to help Marsha because she did not have any spare money to give them! Not even the police officer. She could not afford to take a cab to the American Embassy. Someone at the embassy said they would pay for her transportation when she got there. This turned out to be a lie also. Marsha had to call her mother to wire some money. Della, that woman was never caught or identified. How scary is that? Marsha felt that Customs, the hotel people and the taxis were all working together. With all Marsha's travel experience, she was taken advantage of, in and out. Unbelievable!"

Della didn't get to read even a page of her book since she continued to catch up with Carol the rest of the morning. By the time she got home, Della couldn't tell if she was more depressed hearing about someone else's stupidity or relieved she wasn't the only one on Earth to fall prey.

Wanda called and set up another appointment that evening. Della stared at her bank records for hours, trying to figure out how she was going to get by if the drama wasn't over soon. She thought about getting a housemate but she didn't know who to ask. Everyone in the city knew Della James was an attorney for one of the most acclaimed groups in the South. Della refused to embarrass her family. And asking for a loan was out of the question too since she would have to explain the events to her parents.

Wanda showed up at Della's place an hour early with Chinese food. She was stunned to see the dark circles underneath Della's eyes. "Della, you should know that everybody misses you at work. Now let's get down to business. By the way, you have a lovely home."

"Thank you, Wanda. I liked yours also."

"You know how the proceedings will go. This time I'm the one asking the questions and preparing the arguments and the motions."

Della trusted her. She had no choice. She told her everything about Edward, even the part about their lovemaking. Since they didn't drink this time, Wanda took very accurate notes, only stopping in between to provide a word or two of solace.

Neilmore called to check on Della since she hadn't seen her in a couple weeks. Apparently she'd been doing her own digging because Marlon's name was brought up a few times. "Della, come over after you're finished there with Wanda. I have something I want you to see."

Della found it strange that Neilmore did not say anything about Wanda taking up the case. Had the world turned mad when Edward Dawson stepped into her life? "Neilmore, did I hear you right?"

"What? I said come over when you're finished with Wanda. I had lunch with Marlon today and I want to tell you about our discussion. We're going to help you get through this, baby." Della was mystified that Neilmore wasn't shocked about Wanda stepping into the picture unexpectedly.

Nat King Cole was singing through the CD player at Neilmore's, but neither she nor Della felt like singing along like they always had.

"Neilmore, you look tired. We can do this another time," Della suggested. And she did look tired. The circles under her eyes sprawled around her thick lashes as bad as Della's.

"Nah, from what Marlon told me today at his office, we don't have any time to waste. We've got to clear up the facts that you're not involved with Edward at a conspiratorial level. We don't know how much surveillance has been done on your life this last month, so we need to make sure we cover all your bases and clean your house before they find it dirty."

"Right. But now Wanda's here to make sure of that too."

Neilmore reached for her briefcase and took out a stack of papers. "Yes, but she doesn't have these. Della, do not tell another soul about these documents. All of our careers would be at stake, but blood is thick. Wanda doesn't have that privilege quite yet."

When Della and Neilmore first discussed the potential Patriot Act dynamite that Marlon was fearful could blow Della's career and life to bits, it was Neilmore's usual patience and practicality that kept Della's paranoia to a minimum. It was a dangerous possibility, but many people were cautious of the new Act. Some believed it would strip citizens of their rights. Others were quick to back anything the president touted after September 11th.

"Well, everyone knows that the Patriot Act was hastily and secretly passed by Congress in the name of the war on terrorism just after the World Trade Center was destroyed. It gives the Executive Branch new powers that seriously undermine the Bill of Rights," Neilmore reminded Della. "Are you ready for a quiz?"

"My mind's pretty wasted right now. If you're going to quiz me on the amendments, please just save it and get to the part where my life could be ruined."

Indeed, Neilmore was the all-out scholar of the two. Della sipped on green tea while Neilmore tested her own knowledge. While the government refused to admit it at the time, the Patriot Act most definitely affected the First, Fourth, Fifth, Sixth, Eighth, and Fourteenth Amendments. Freedoms of religion, speech, assembly and the press were being swayed, along with freedom from unreasonable searches and seizures. As if that weren't enough, during Della's time of crisis, the right to a speedy public trial by an impartial jury would be shaky as well.

"Della, stop gaping at me and tell me what the Fourteenth is and how it applies to you."

"Okay, teacher, all persons—citizens and non-citizens within the United States are entitled to due process and equal protection of the laws."

"Now, that's worth every cent your Mama and Daddy spent in Harvard Law dollars."

Della rolled her eyes. "Yeah, but I'm not as up on this Patriot Act as you are apparently. I still don't understand how it will have the power to screw me senseless if the elusive Edward Dawson doesn't come correct."

There were four really scary areas. One, the U.S. Patriot Act had expanded terrorism laws to include "domestic terrorism," which could subject political organizations to surveillance, wiring tapping, harassment and criminal action for political advocacy. Two, it expanded the ability of law enforcement to conduct secret searches, giving them wide powers of phone and Internet surveillance, and access to highly personal medical, financial, mental health and student records with minimal judicial oversight. Three, it allowed F.B.I. agents to investigate citizens for criminal matters without probable cause of crime if they claimed it was for "intelligence purposes."

The most daunting area was that it permitted non-citizens to be jailed based on mere suspicion and to be denied readmission to the States for engaging in free speech. Convicted suspects could be detained indefinitely in six-month increments without meaningful judicial review.

"Della, there are convicted suspects who have been detained at Guantanamo Bay for a year and haven't seen the light of day, much less had a trial yet."

When the American Civil Liberties Union swiftly organized concerned citizens to protest the Act, Neilmore had gotten involved. She wrote letters and attended several meetings to get Atlanta's city officials to reject it and to inform Capitol Hill that the country was not pleased with their idea of national security.

Both Neilmore and Della reflected on what kind of system they actually worked for. "Neilmore, am I, is Marlon, wrong to be paranoid?"

"Not really, but I say it's better to be proactive than paranoid, okay? Marlon's main concern is probably based on the fact Edward impersonated a pilot and that if by chance the Feds are onto Edward, you could be on their 'terrorism' radar screen too." Just expect a special investigator or agent from the department of defense homeland security to be at our door.

"My nerves are so shot." Della jumped up to make two of her famously strong martinis.

"Naturally they're shot, baby. But all we have to do is keep being thankful for Marlon giving us a heads-up. I know you've seen all these documents related to Edward Dawson, but I copied them so we'll be well-prepared if everything comes down on you. We have to make sure there's nothing the Feds will find on you to whisk you away to Guantanamo Bay."

The thought was unreal. "Neilmore, you never cease to amaze me. You went to Marlon to get access to all this, and he gave it to you? How do you keep outshining yourself?"

"You mean by drinking your strong-ass martinis and talking law at the same time without slurring?" She waited for Della to laugh, a sure sign that some of her worries were gone, and when she did, Neilmore continued. "You know that Marlon is a wonderful man and he will do anything to help you, Della. It was not hard to get a copy of everything that's come across that man's desk in the last few weeks. He's waiting for your call."

"What do you mean he's waiting for my call?"

That's right, Marlon was waiting on Della's call. She had promised to return to his office weeks ago, but seeing Edward's face all over the room in toothy mug shots absolutely turned her stomach. She had shared all she knew. And now like Neilmore and Marlon, Wanda too had all the dreadful details of how Della had been played. What more was there to say?

CHAPTER Twenty-two

Della sat outside Marlon's office praying for a strong heart. After two martinis, Neilmore had convinced Della to see Marlon the next day. He kissed Della on the cheek as she sat in that same listless white room that closed in around her once before. Mercifully, Marlon did not mention her stupid mistake of allowing Edward to escape. She listened as he discussed the next move of the authorities. Della wondered about Jamie but didn't mention her.

"Dirty son of a bishop without good sermons. Do you see this sucker's *modus operandi*, Marlon? He targets single career women of color!"

"Yep, Della, it's obvious. Thing is, now you've got to jump on this sucker. How are you dealing with being out of work?"

"I'm going to string him up by his feet, roast him

that way for a few days in the sun and tell all the neighborhood kids he's a piñata."

"No, Della, seriously. Are you okay?"

"Seriously? I'm going to wash his hands in honey and set loose a swarm of African killer bees on him before I tell everyone in the neighborhood he's a piñata."

"Della, I'm very worried about you," Marlon said gently. He knew she had a great sense of humor but so far, Della had not allowed him to know how she had really been the last few weeks. He could only imagine. "Della, are we friends again? I miss your sharp diva-fied wit!"

"I guess." Della tried to make humility fit. "By the way, and just so you know, even though I didn't come to the wedding and have never accepted your invitations to the anniversary parties, I've been fine with you and Jamie being together. It's just that I feel that she still wants to demolish me after all these years."

Della always had a hard time throwing the gauntlet down – *once Della's, always Della's*, wasn't that how she declared it herself – and Marlon knew Jamie taking the reigns irked her, but he wasn't going to touch that with a baseball bat.

Marlon knew it. Jamie had been a little rough on Della, even in front of the family. Marlon thought

back on the box he and Jamie received from Sothe-
by's with the pair of Beijing vases Della sent one year
as a wedding gift. He recalled how Jamie's joy vanished when she read the card inside and realized it
had been signed by Della.

Marlon had hoped the hatchet and ill will between the sisters could be forever buried. Looking
at Jamie's face as she read the card and noticing how
those vases disappeared from their home, he knew
there was more work to do.

Just as she was about to leave, Della asked sincerely how things were at home and Marlon mumbled, "We're… she's… she's… Della, I think Jamie's
having an affair."

Della could not believe her ears. She sat in the car
for the longest time trying to figure out how to ap-
proach Jamie. At this point in the Edward episode,
she would have to connect with her anyway. It was
clear that the authorities were about to contact everyone affiliated with Della James. She knew her sister
would freak. Or would she secretly glow in the light
of baby sister's scandalous existence? Della didn't
know anymore. When Marlon disclosed all the mystery surrounding Jamie's sporadic trips to Canada
to tend to an old friend who was in the middle of
a divorce, it was obvious on his face that he didn't

believe her. *But an affair?* Della would have never guessed Jamie to be capable of it.

Just as she was getting settled in on the highway with the new Beyonce CD, her cell phone rang. Wanda's number came up. She hesitated to pick it up, but decided there would be no time to rest until "the drama" (she and Neilmore billed this time period) was completely over.

"Della, the Feds were at the firm today. They walked into your office barely saying a word to Jeremy and turned on your computer. I'm sure they copied the entire hard drive. Then they went into Jeremy's office with a box of your files. We have got to put our heads together, this is happening so fast."

"So, now it's all coming down, huh?" Beyonce was bouncing in the background.

"Look, Della, you know our firm can deal with the district attorney's office. We have friends there – and family, yes – but to deal with the federal government in a tribunal is too costly."

"What are you telling me? The firm could be held suspect if they did not cooperate?"

"It's more than that, Della. Everyone around you could be questioned and be subject to unprecedented subpoena powers of the federal government."

All Della could think about was her family. She

could deal with the monetary loss, but this was too much. "That son of a bitch!"

There was no avoiding the inevitable. She would have to tell Jamie before someone unpleasant did.

"Della, do you have any idea what he would do with your money? Sounds insane, but he could use it to buy pharmaceuticals, weapons, or help finance some other criminal activity." Like Neilmore, Wanda demonstrated that she'd gotten personally involved to try to interrupt the passing of the Patriot Act. "Let's calm down. If they really wanted you, the Feds could have come straight to your house again. It's been weeks."

CHAPTER *Twenty-three*

A fter watching two reruns of "Soul Food" and dab-
bling with her watercolors, Della mustered up
enough courage to call Jamie on her cell phone. She
would only give her a briefing and not ask any questions about Marlon.

Della kept the conversation to a minimum despite
her burning curiosity about what her sister was up
to, if there was even a distraught friend in Canada or
if she was sleeping with the architect of her dreams
once and for all.

Della told Jamie all about Edward, day one until
now, how she was over at Neilmore's trying to get
things straight just in case Edward had brought the
F.B.I down on the family and her friends.

"Jamie, I have a feeling that you'll be the first they
contact."

"No shit?" Jamie was tapping her nails on the dining room table. Della sensed it.

"Yes, I'm ashamed to say it's true. They could be searching for terrorist information. This is deep."

"You know why would I damn near expect anything different from you? How are you going to get out of this one, hot-ass? You know what? I can't deal with this issue right now. I was about to make myself some tea and go to bed. Let me think about this and call you tomorrow."

Della did not have a chance to respond before Jamie set the phone down. Jamie was outraged. She thought about going for a long drive instead of hitting the sack, but she was getting tired of lying to Marlon.

"Who was that calling so late, baby J?" Marlon peeped in from the living room.

"That was your crazy sister-in-law. Talking about some lousy investigation. She thought I already knew about it. Why did she think that, Marlon?" She brushed past him wide-eyed, cutting off whatever he was about to say.

"Marlon, I'm tired. I'm going to bed. You don't have to follow." Jamie scampered past Marlon's home office, noting that he was still logged into the main database. Soon, Marlon heard the bedroom door shut loudly. He knew he had a lot of explaining to do and could have reamed Della for not giving him notice she was going to finally tell Jamie.

Jamie felt like a time bomb quivering to explode. She had not expected things to get so out of control. An F.B.I. investigation? Impossible. Like as before "Edward Dawson" had walked into their lives, Jamie blamed Della on everything – even her own intentions. It was a sick cycle and she knew she had to bring an end to it.

Within a week that Wanda predicted, Della received her summons to superior court and the judicial bar hearing. She was ready. Della and Wanda jokingly kept referring to love victimization, but damn it, that's what had happened to her in her eyes.

Since Della's case with the superior court was under Title Three, Wanda could motion for dismissal and claim rights of discovery, only answering what was in her area of law. She had completed loads of research and had prepared her oral argument smoothly. Wanda knew the necessary depositions to take. As they went over it during hot pancakes that morning, she would prove Della was simply a victim of love and certainly not a part of an international intelligence operation dealing with terrorism.

The judge had been impressed by the Goldberg firm for years, and he was probably easier to deal with than other Southern judges. The case was called into a preliminary hearing and the charges of obstructing justice were moved on to a trial court. Within the trial court, Della was sentenced to two months in jail since she had no prior criminal record. That sentence was then condensed into one hundred volunteer hours for a city literacy program, thanks to Wanda's tough reasoning.

Next came the judicial bar hearing, where Della thought she was going to faint from embarrassment. "Della, get a hold of yourself. I need you to be stern, emotional but stern," Wanda insisted.

As predicted, the investigators did not have enough material against her that would warrant taking away her license. The man that she kept referring to, "Edward Dawson" was still nowhere to be found. Instead, the association suspended her for three months as a result of the criminal trial.

CHAPTER *Twenty-four*

Edward was in Vancouver *laying low and spending dough*, laughing off his last sting, a young Black doctor in Chicago he convinced to invest $50,000 in a scam deal without her husband's knowledge. Sure, she was familiar with the new drug Edward had a hot tip was due in days to clear the Federal Drug Administration approved list. It would definitely shoot through the roof as the Viagra for women. Dr. Robinson came through like a champ for Edward.

In Vancouver, Edward was high on himself. He could have been a wealthy man many times over but Edward worked his game to keep it tight, and in between games lived the easy money out, enjoying the best of everything.

Quite by coincidence, Edward had stumbled upon an architecture convention months ago that was taking place in the hotel. Attracted by the high number of distinguished Black women he saw in the meetings, he made it a point to mingle at the bar each evening.

He met a charming woman from Atlanta. She had studied architecture but was not an architect. They had several drinks and chatted way past midnight. She was married to the county district attorney. Edward was very interested in architecture, having invested in renovated properties around five major cities in the States. Additionally, he owned lots of property around the world but considered himself a casual realtor. The woman's father was seriously into real estate too.

Edward needed to tell someone about his crazy life and this sexy stranger would do. He mentioned his wayward cousin, the conman. How he had no conscience. How he'd go to work on young Black professional women and how his game was irresistibly tight. How he confided in Edward because they looked like twins and had been best friends since childhood. Maybe Edward was the only legitimate friend in the world his cousin could trust. Damn fool had the nerve to ask him to see what he could do among his rich friends to get his con record cleaned up.

They laughed at the cousin's escapades. She told Edward, almost jokingly, how she knew someone she'd love to see his cousin tighten up, just for the hell of it. Then, because there was an early session the next morning, the woman from Atlanta said goodnight. If Edward ever ventured to Atlanta, he would be sure to give her a call.

Edward was so high on himself that night, he paid the tab. The next evening, she spotted him at the club. "I found you again, what a nice surprise," she said with a spark in her eyes. They ditched the dance floor and took a bottle of wine to the lounge area.

"You seem to be a nice man, Edward. What is on your mind?"

"Oh, quite a lot. Business is slow and I don't trust my family," he replied. They both chuckled through unfeigned drunkenness. "Other than that, the world is a lonely place and you're a married woman."

Jamie thought about the statement long and hard. "Yes, I am married. He's a wonderful man." They stared at their wineglasses absentmindedly. "But that doesn't mean you and I won't be of value to each other."

He took in the massive cleavage of her breasts and nodded in approval. They spoke of their naughtiest natures for five hours before Jamie returned to her hotel room. He had given her four different numbers so they could keep very close touch over the coming months. Everything was secured that fateful night.

CHAPTER *Twenty-five*

SPRING 2002

Edward expected her. He complemented how beautiful she was dressed. "Well, this is a special evening."

"Oh? Well, my real point is that you fill out a dress better than your sister any day," he said thickly. It was a small pleasure for Jamie, having fuller breasts than Della. She looked exquisite in the scooped neck lavender silk cocktail dress and the flowing scarf. Everything matched perfectly from her boots to her pearl earrings.

Edward had barely taken the bottle of white wine from her hands before she was undressing him, kissing him wildly. She backed him up to one of the spacious beds. Jamie was unrelenting. Between kisses, he tried to call her name.

"Jamie!" She was all over him, unbuttoning him, unzipping him over his bulge. "Jamie, this is so unlike you! What has gotten into you?" Edward thought that was all he needed—to have sex with a county district attorney's wife after they both scammed her sister.

"Edward, oh Edward, you sweet, sexy devil, you." She rubbed him with a gentle forcefulness and laid another long, juicy kiss on him. "Take a shower while I pour the wine," she commanded in a purr. He obeyed.

Jamie was naked when he returned, sprawled across the bedcovers, offering wine. She offered a toast and talked. "Edward, you handled your last assignment so well, I may have something else for you."

"Now, that's the Jamie I need to know." He was beginning to relax and wanted to talk about more money. Edward tensed again though when she began fingering the knot in his bathrobe.

"This is an excellent wine, huh?" She took a huge swallow.

Edward did too. "Oh, very twangy but interesting." Minutes later, Edward Dawson was slumped over on the bed, looking like a toppled over Buddha statue. His breath turned light and even in no time.

The horse tranquilizer would suit him just fine for a while.

Edward Dawson was born as Ronald Nettleford, the oldest of five children. His mother told him that he was conceived through rape. She said that she had been on a tourist bus that broke down just outside the city. When the other riders went for help, she stayed behind with the driver and a young Italian tourist. The two men overpowered her and raped her.

Edward never really felt loved by his mother. Despite his ongoing façade with women, his subconscious represented a dark hole of grief. He did not hate women, however. On the contrary, Edward adored them. He adored them so much that he wanted to help them be aware of their weaknesses. He felt that he deserved their money, their love, and their time. Edward possessed the advantage that most men did not have, as he could respond to every move a person made. Through interactive programming exercises, Edward had learned to develop a rapport with everyone. He was a master of linguistic programming, understanding the connection between feeling and mental effectiveness. There were no mental blocks that he could not break through to make a woman feel that by being with him, she was bettering herself.

After leaving the confines of a poor, unstable home, Edward Dawson set out to show the world what true success looked like. And he used women to validate that plan. No, they were not his mother but they were of the same feeble kind, according to the voice that spoke to him every morning.

Through it all, however, Della James had finally represented something different. Even as Edward took her money and littered her life with misfortune like all the others, he could not shake the realization that love had finally found him. Della would never truly know, so there was nothing left to do besides carry on with his irreversible plan.

CHAPTER Twenty-six

A ll signs of Jamie were gone. Had she even been there in the first place? Edward's head felt huge and heavy. His vision teetered from one side of the room to the other in a haze. He pushed himself off the bed with all the strength he could draw from his brawny arms. Edward stumbled around the room, forcing his legs to carry him. Every distance was further away then it seemed.

The clothes were gone. His personal belongings were gone. The phone line was cut through. Edward was stark naked and so was the hotel room. There were no drapes, towels, no shower curtain, no bedspread, and no linen. There was nothing but a letter taped to the mirror that read: "You've been played!" Edward snorted like a wild beast.

"I hadn't even had my toast or tea of the morning, man," the desk clerk explained to the detectives. "I look up and there is a man in his birthday suit." The clerk giggled at the thought of it while Marlon Richards gestured for him to hurry up about Edward's whereabouts. "I didn't intend any disrespect. I'm sorry. I realize this is serious business but just thinking about it again makes me laugh. What a way to start the workday, huh?" He did not know where Edward was heading in the hotel's employee uniform they provided for him.

"After he told me he'd been robbed, I calmed him down and gave him a sheet to cover himself. I offered to call the police but he refused. He wanted me to write the police station's address down and said that he would file a report later. He had some important meeting that he had to get to. It didn't make sense to me, a professional like that not wanting to at least report his credit cards stolen and protect his assets right away. Pearl, the other clerk, and I found a doorman suit and shoes. He was pissed he had to wear that, but at least we assisted him!"

Edward was born a survivor, someone so sly, he could con the pope out of the money in the offering bowl if he wanted to. He knew he would find a suit his size if the customer service rep could be charmed. Edward strolled into the cleaners in his doorman suit with the Wapiti Hotel emblem on the pocket. He spotted one clerk from outside, a young-ish woman thankfully.

When she asked politely how could she help him, Edward said he came for the suit and the pressed shirts for hotel customers who must have confused him for the meek errand boy. The girl giggled and blushed. He did not have the cleaning tickets but could identify the clothes. Could she please check? Edward convinced the girl that he would go back to the hotel to get the tickets, but he wanted to know if the clothes were ready. After all, these were execu-tives that he had to please. "Miss, I especially need the pinstriped one that's 40" long with a matching white shirt." Sure there were a few of them he could eyeball if she agreed to spin the carousel.

Edward memorized a number and when he was sure the clothes carousel would stop with the num-ber at the rear of the cleaners, he asked the clerk to stop. It was no use. He'd go back. But wait, he thought he remembered the big red numbers on the ticket. He casually called out the seven digits. When she obliged by walking to the back to check, Edward swiped a pinstripe suit and a few shirts aggressively off the rack. He made off for his important meeting.

"That'll be fine, Mr. Dawson. When you recover your documents, Fed Ex them and that will be all.

How, in fact, did you come to lose the papers anyway?"

"I'd rather not discuss the details until I talk with
the police. I'm going there straight from here." Edward sounded very convincing.

"Vancouver is usually more kind to guests, Mr.
Dawson. I am sorry for your inconvenience." She
glanced back at the file on the conference room table.
"Now if you could sign here…" Edward signed and
she flipped the pages. "And here, that will finish the
paperwork necessary before I can walk this down to
accounting. We'll then go over the final transaction
quickly, photocopy everything, and you'll be out of
here soon."

Edward signed. He was extremely pleased with
himself.

"Can I have someone bring you a cup of tea, coffee, anything while you wait?"

Edward shook his head *no thanks*. "Well, then, it
won't be long before you can go to the police and
make your report. I'll be back." Heading for the accounting department, the woman left Edward smiling over his accomplishments. He wasn't dazed and
confused any longer either. *That bitch!* Edward kept
the smile in spite of his anger at Jamie Richards.

CHAPTER Twenty-seven

Marlon had flown to Vancouver in search of Jamie. He had no idea how he would respond to seeing his wife of ten years with another man, not to mention a crook he'd been investigating for the last year. And Della? Marlon geared up thinking of the pain she'd endured.

The front desk clerk could not identify Jamie as the woman in the picture, but Marlon knew Jamie had been in Vancouver. The man Marlon put on the plane with Jamie had followed her every move. No doubt staring at her fine ass the entire time, but he had reported every step to Marlon, nonetheless. It infuriated Marlon to know that Jamie had erased Edward's records out the system in his office and shredded his files. Neilmore and Della had only a fragment of the copied documents that he needed to try the bastard. And the worst part was the affair that made his heart ache.

A handsome man in a pinstriped suit had entered the stately suite of offices. The brass signature overwhelming the granite wall behind the reception area read "Valentine Investments of Vancouver, Ltd." Edward appreciated how the suite's granite and chrome modernity played off the elegance of the historic building he walked into. Even if he hoped no one noticed his cheap shoes, Edward was secure in his character and snapped into his role right away.

"Good morning," he charmed the receptionist. "I'm Edward Dawson. I'd give you my card but I have had the great misfortune this morning of misplacing my wallet." He was expected and right on time for his appointment with Mrs. Valentine.

Edward sought refuge for his shoes by sitting on the couch behind a coffee table. Someone brought him aspirin and water promptly as he had asked. His head was killing him. He took the letter from his inside jacket pocket and read it again for the fifth time. Jamie had gotten to his luggage, expensive clothes, wallet, even the drapes for good measure in hopes of adding the expense to his hotel bill. However, she had not gotten the wet bath towel off the floor where Della's signed loan papers were tucked under. Thank sweet Jesus, Edward thought a million times during that hour of inconvenience.

Della came through. It was a pretty good finishing touch to lay on her that day at the bank. The rainy day plan was an old move but it was far from dead. Worked like a charm! After all those gifts, Della was unwilling to budge at the bank. She couldn't just up and give $35,000 in cash, but $20,000 would have to suffice. She could help in other ways to make up for the difference in the next day or two. She had the dough! She could have done whatever she wanted, but pressing the issue would not have been wise. So it had to be the rainy day plan. There was property in Vancouver she could buy and put him down as co-owner. They'd be getting married anyway, wouldn't they? He could borrow off that as the collateral he needed to get a sure money deal off the ground. That would hold him until he could straighten his assets out. The sooner, the better.

Edward's headache made him grind his teeth. The aspirin wasn't cutting through the pounding. *Why is the other property co-owner Jamie James Richards? Must be one of Della's legal tricks. The woman was smart, that's for sure. The dollar amount is five times more than I expected.* Edward could definitely live with that.

A young Black femme fatale walked across the reception area with pep and flair toward Edward.

"Mr. Dawson? Good morning. I'm Natalie Valentine, President of Valentine Investments."

Standing to shake Natalie's hand, Edward thinks, *just my type.*

"Come with me, Mr. Dawson. I'm sorry for your wait. I have some papers for you to sign and you'll soon be on your way. Please follow me. My assistant told me that someone took your wallet. How terrible!"

Marlon identified himself and the two men with him as Atlanta Police Department undercover detectives. The clerk cooperated. She hadn't seen so many handsome Black men in one day.

No, the clerk had never seen the woman in the picture. Yes, Pearl remembered the man who checked into Room 1109 as Edward Bonneau. He had mentioned he was a realtor in town for a meeting with his Canadian investor. The office was right down the street in the plushest building on the block. No one could miss it. "Mr. Bonneau is wearing the hotel's doorman suit. It's all we could do for him." Pearl laughed like a hyena.

Marlon walked into Valentine Investments of Vancouver, Ltd. with the other men and the receptionist cooperated. It had been perfect timing, a detective's wet dream.

Mrs. Valentine's partner escorted Marlon and

the men in the opposite direction of the conference room where Edward was meeting with her. The man showed them to an office and manipulated the high-tech speakerphone.

"Okay, Mr. Richards, you're set. It's on mute, so you could theoretically have a party in here and nobody on the other side of the line would know. They're just getting started."

The man closed the door behind them quietly. They listened, barely taking a breath.

Not quite thirty minutes later, Jamie marched up to the Valentine reception desk and asked to see Mrs. Valentine. She was asked to take a seat. Meantime, the receptionist buzzed Marlon and alerted the detectives to take their positions. "Mrs. Richards, someone will be out in just a second to take you to the conference room. Ms. Valentine will join you and Mr. Dawson there shortly."

Soon, Jamie remained standing at the opposite end of a long conference table where Edward was seated. Jamie had surveyed the conference room in enclosed glass with two entrances. She would not have gone in otherwise. There was corridor traffic—someone pushing a mail cart, someone running to make copies—and she felt safe with that knowledge. Jamie had no idea how angry Edward was or what he was capable of doing.

"Nice suit, Edward," Jamie laughed dramatically.

To Jamie's surprise, Edward almost looked dormant. "I knew you had a cold streak running through you, Jamie, but what was that incident about? Where's my wallet?"

"Just a minor inconvenience, Edward. What's this all about?" Jamie waved the Valentine Investment letter at him. She had seen and copied it, after all.

Edward would keep his cool, even though he was completely shocked.

"Oh, yes, if you were a course, you'd pass minor inconvenience at the top of your class, classless loser that you are."

"I may be all that, but I bet you won't pull this one off, you scoundrel. You had an assignment and I paid you for it. On that note, Della paid you well too, the stupid bitch she was. I even cleared your records out of the system because you took that assignment too far–I told you my husband's a district attorney, for cryin' out loud! The Feds will tie me to you. I only wanted you to shake Della up a bit, not con her out of all her money and threaten her career! You rat, you thank me by trying to scam me? I won't let you get away with it." Jamie had known all along there was no cousin. Edward was a very desperate, lonely man. Always had been, and she saw him for what he was.

Edward gloated. "My dear, I am waiting, as you rage, for the check so I can laugh all the way to the bank. Della was good for many things. Maybe you should follow suit."

Jamie was floored. "How do you plan on cashing it without a wallet?"

"Step off the big screen, Ms. Minor. I will manage. And scam you? This is icing on the delicious Della deal. I don't know why she put your name on this deal, but I figured it's a cutthroat sister streak that runs in the family."

Jamie was speechless. She couldn't figure out why Della had put her name down either. A safety net? At this point, Jamie couldn't worry about that detail but it was obvious that Della had fiddled with her secretly as well. She wondered what else her name was on.

"And as for your act," Edward continued nastily, "you wanted to seduce me to drug me and rip me off, that earned you an award for the Petties, Ms. Minor."

"I wouldn't cheat on my man for anything and, if my life depended on it, not with a low life like you. And let me tell you one more thing. If someone walks in here with a check without me signing off on anything, there's going to be a lot more hell than this morning, Edward - or is that even your name – asshole."

Just then, Mrs. Valentine entered the conference room on Jamie's side. With the file under her arm, she extended a handshake to Jamie. "Mrs. Richards, I am Natalie Valentine." She immediately turned to Edward. "I apologize, Mr. Dawson. In an oversight, due to the fact that my vice president usually handles this part of transactions, I forgot to get Mrs. Richard's signatures. Accounting won't do a thing without them.

It was time for Jamie to gloat. "Mrs. Valentine, I am sorry but I will not be signing *anything*."

Edward stood abruptly to leave when the detectives entered through both the conference room doors to arrest him. The office was a scurry of inquiries about the scandal.

CHAPTER Twenty-eight

Outside in a lot behind Valentine Investments, Marlon approached Edward in cuffs. "So how does it feel to get chumped, chump?" Edward had nothing to say. "Cat got your tongue? I can see how swallowing your own medicine might do that, man. So get this, I'll talk and tell you no lies. Player, you are going for a plane ride back to your roots. Now, I'm kind of certain that you'll never get off that island again, so I suggest you find another trade and get your act together, although personally I don't give a damn about you. You obviously played with the wrong family, player!"

Edward found his voice. "I know my rights and I'm not saying anything until I talk to an attorney. Who in the hell are you anyway?"

"Oh, where are my manners? I'm Marlon Richards, District Attorney, Atlanta. Jamie's my wife."

Marlon signaled to the detectives that he was through talking to Edward. "By the way, man," Marlon said to Edward as he attempted to situate his long legs in the backseat of the unmarked car, "nice shoes."

Although the office was still abuzz with news of the arrest floating over the phone wires between office workers, things were much calmer and the corridors were clear of spectators.

"Marlon?!" Jamie interrupted Mrs. Valentine, who had been telling her about the origin of the investment. "Marlon, what are you doing here?" He stood against the door with his arms folded.

"No, Jamie, that's my question. And since this is official business, I expect an answer. What are you doing here?"

Mrs. Valentine excused herself. She thought *This would sure be enough fodder to go around the company for the rest of the week.*

Jamie's mind stumbled for an answer. She hadn't a clue where to begin or what could soften the blow for everyone involved... even Della. "Marlon, I... I... I..."

"Jamie, do you realize I could have you arrested for tampering with classified files?" He moved in much closer to her now.

"But Marlon, we can talk about it all at home, I..."

Marlon stopped Jamie from backing away by pulling her to him gently.

"Or put you on probation for tampering with my heart."

Edward was hardly amused by the vast stretch of clouds sauntering through fans of sunlight. He was disgusted. How he hated returning to Jamaica after six years. Jamaica would still be an island surviving barely on tourist dollars and most of the poor people, no matter how hard they worked, would still serve the hotels and the resorts. It would not be enough for him, ever. He kept the handcuffs covered with the pinstriped jacket and ordered a drink. "How about a whiskey sour?" *In honor of Della James.*

Edward could have been thinking about people he left behind and would soon be seeing again—his mother, brothers and sisters, the librarian Mrs. Dunn, the beach bums at the Royal Jamaican Weight Club. He could have been thinking about festivals or carnivals zipping with huge fruits and fished in the Black hands of machete-wielding mamas talking fast to make a sale, caressed by the oranges and pinks of sunrise and sunset, diamond skies and harvest moons. Instead, Edward thought of sun-baked dirt roads and shanties, underfed chickens and droopy-drawered barefoot kids kicking up dirt.

When he could catch the stewardess, Edward Dawson would have another double.

"Jamie…?" Jamie nodded *yes* as Marlon continued. She was so sorry, so very sorry, tears poured down her mocha-skinned face.

"We're going to do things right from here on out. When we get home, we are going to put this behind us."

Jamie had no idea what Marlon was talking about. She nearly ruined Della's life, the family's reputation, and her marriage. She chalked it up that she would never be able to put the past year behind her, as Della would want to kill her. And finally, Jamie did not blame her. "Marlon, I would never cheat on you. Please believe me. I am a rotten person for jeopardizing my sister's life, but I promise I will never hurt another soul. Does Della know? Oh god!" Jamie crumbled onto the floor, releasing tears that she never knew she had even. They were large pleas for forgiveness.

"Jamie, I don't expect everything to heal when we get off that plane, but if you can say you're willing to work at it, that's good enough for me. Pull yourself together, Della does not know. … And I will never tell her." Jamie reached for Marlon's leg like a wounded animal. She'd never felt so grateful or full of love in her life. Marlon pulled her up off the floor. "But first, we have to make some conditions."

Marlon did not want to go home worrying about when Jamie was going to snap again. He would go to therapy with her, the family didn't have to know. He did not want to have to remember who not to invite to their anniversary parties nor turn any gifts down. Jamie would have to accept that he still loved Della just like he loved Neilmore—as sisters.

CHAPTER *Twenty-nine*

Della decided to attend church again. She had not been to a church in over a year. Della craved some spiritual words, something to fill her up at least for the day, so she went to a church on the corner from her house. The church nearly ran over with people, it was so popular. Della sat in the back. Within minutes, a tall, white-haired minister addressed the crowd and brought everyone to their feet for the greeting. He held up the Bible and everyone sat back down.

"I know some of you are going through something in your life today. It's going to be all right. Put yourself in line with God's best. When you explore God's best, you explore your best. This is because he made you for a purpose. Most human beings live and die without exercising their maximum potential. God is not lazy. He has done everything for us. He has made us all independently connected, but still mutually exclusive. You must take personal initiative and ask yourself this question, 'What is it that I have to give?' What can I give life?' the Creator says, 'I did so much already, I gave you a brain. You figure out what it is you're supposed to do with it.

"Don't let personal disappointments derail you. The fullness of God's power is in you, and he will make everything possible for you to overcome. He said, 'Do something for me. Put me first and give me the acknowledgement I deserve. There is nothing you can't have. I own everything and everybody. Your time will not be wasted, and you will achieve your full potential. You will accomplish your purpose in a meaningful life. When you let down your guard because of loneliness, and seek people behind your emotions instead of common sense, you are bound to be let down.

"We sharpen our skills in pain and learn better in peace. When we take responsibility for ourselves, then we are on the right track. Our problems lie in how we think and what we want. We lose ourselves in the things or people we believe that we should have. Your best friend may let you down, but loving God won't. Never want anyone so bad that you sacrifice what you stand for just to have them. You may never know a person after being with them for years. People are full of surprises, so don't get upset with disappointments."

Della had heard enough, so she quietly exited through the side door. It wasn't that she was unimpressed. In contrast, she was utterly beside herself with tears. As the tears mingled with Della's eye makeup, the stinging became unbearable. Even as she washed her face in the privacy of her bathroom, those tears did not stop.

CHAPTER Thirty

Months had passed. Wanda Durham helped Della survive the fight of her life. She had painted several landscapes and even saw Dr. Venus a few times. Jamie, who was now happily pregnant, had taken her out to lavish dinners to reconnect with her. There was noticeably a change in her older sister, that was for sure. She didn't care what the source of the generosity was, maybe pity on her, but it seemed strange at first. And yet, Della was still very depressed. She felt a deep longing in her heart. This time she did not recognize it as a longing for a man or relationship. There was something more profound missing. Soon, Della was scheduled to go back to Goldberg as well, but another calling waited in the shadows.

One Saturday afternoon, Wanda dropped by. "I just came to see you after all we went through. I'm sorry I haven't been in touch, but the cases have occupied all of my time. I will be glad when you come back to the firm!" She embraced Della lovingly.

"I'm thankful for all your help. I hope that I will be able to repay you one day," Della said weakly.

"You certainly will, and not in dollars mind you." They both laughed. Besides food and a few books to keep her mind off the past, Della had not spent much money. She was learning for the first time in her life to do without products, trips, plays, and even hair appointments. I stopped by to invite you on a journey. You don't have to pay for anything… just let me show you a good time."

Della didn't respond right away. "Wanda, you should let me show you a good time. I haven't been out dancing in a while. How about it next weekend?"

"That sounds good." said Wanda.

"Well, you will come back to the firm, right?" Wanda asked, sensing that Della was really neutral.

"Of course, what makes you think I wouldn't?"

"I just want to make sure you're ready next week. We're really counting on you. You're a damned good attorney. There, I said it!"

Della nodded in approval and walked Wanda out to her car.

That week, Edward Dawson was consulted by an investigator to be advised of his international rights by a tribunal. Edward was convicted of international conspiracy, polygamy, forgery, and associated charges compounded by international laws. He was sentenced to fifty years in prison at an unknown location. After serving only two weeks, Edward initiated a brawl with a radical extremist inmate who damaged his kidney. His kidney became infected, resulting in a disease that caused him to lose weight and his memory. Before the tragedy, Edward was already suffering a great loss.

In truth, he had fallen in love with Della, but it was too late. He would live the rest of his life in sorrow for what he had done to her and his wives who loved him. When he was not thinking of Della, Edward thought of his home in Jamaica to soothe his nerves. He wished he could have shared the fading memories with her. He did not have a Jamaican accent but could speak *Patois* when necessary. This was something that he had wanted Della to know, but never got to tell her. Edward had fantasized about her seeing Ranway Bay, Negril and Port Antonio. He wanted to spill champagne all over her body near the ocean. If Della could have seen the Jamaican sun and felt the warm breeze, she would have possessed no stress.

Edward felt like he knew Della's faults: greed and arrogance. To understand any woman Edward knew it was a matter of chemistry. If the chemistry and pheromones fused, all you had to do was play it right and use the attraction for your advantage. He was pleased with himself for mastering the game before wallowing in his own demise.

CHAPTER Thirty-one

"Sometimes you can exploit yourself by not taking the proper time to get all the facts about a person before you make a decision. Temptation can come into your life just to sidetrack you away from your dream, your purpose and knowing yourself."

As she sat in church again and again each week, Della collected his words in her mental treasure chest. They held meaning and power.

Della enjoyed the minister's message so much, she took home a stack of pamphlets of his writings. She had been uplifted tremendously just in that hour, and she was pleased with herself for attending the service. The words were meant for her, she was convinced. Now it was time to do something with the impression sealed in her heart. But what? Della poured over the minister's messages alongside a cup of tea.

Della was determined to turn her life around. She had always lived using her conventional knowledge to judge people and the world, and she failed. Now she was ready to turn to God for help. Della communicated that she could not make it on her own. With tears in her eyes she raised her hands to ask for God's help. She vowed to go to bed and wake up an entirely different person.

As she climbed the stairs to the hallway, Della felt the soft cool wind in the hallway. The air was filled with sweet roses. It was unlike any garden smell. A feeling of enormous relief came over Della. She paused, waiting for the music of peace to play on the stereo. It did not blare through the speakers, it revealed in her heart.

CHAPTER Thirty-two

The first day back at work was the best for Della. Life was beginning to return to normal as she was reminiscing of the past, then a call was transferred to her.

"This is attorney Della James, how can I help you?"

My name is Mary Banks. Miss James I'm in trouble I don't understand. I got in trouble at the airport. I had a BB gun in my suitcase, and I did not know it was there. I told security at the airport I was sorry and they took the replica BB gun but now I'm being charged anyway. I received a letter from the U.S. Department of Homeland Security office on Inspections regarding the incident.

"What did it say?"

It said,

"It is a violation of 49 Code of Federal Regulations (CFR) Section 1540.111(a)(1) for an unauthorized person to have a weapon, explosive, or incendiary, on or about the individual's person or accessible property while inside, or attempting to enter, an airport sterile area once the screening process has begun. A sterile area is that part of an airport between the security checkpoint and the passenger gate. Violation of these regulations could carry a civil penalty under the provisions of Title 49, United States Code, Section 46301 as amended by the Homeland Security Act of 2002.

The investigation substantiated that a lifelike replica firearm is considered a dangerous weapon in a sterile area. We have given careful consideration to all available facts and have concluded that this matter does not warrant legal enforcement action. In lieu of such action, we are issuing this notice of warning, which is being made a matter of record. We expect your future compliance with the regulations."

"Miss Banks they are closing the case."

I know but I got another letter from the city attorney's office saying a complaint has been filed in violation of Section P171-BA6 which says posses a pellet gun in a state or park building. What shall I do?

"Miss Banks go to the hearing. Do you have a clean record?"

Yes. I don't have any tickets or anything.

"Good. Be there early. This is just an office hearing. You can go pro- per by representing yourself. Just tell the truth and how sorry you are and it should work out fine for you."

Thank you so much Miss James for your advice.

Della felt good to be back at work looking over the city behind the dark tinted windows. However, she knew in the near future she would have her own law firm.

Epilogue

People wait in the reception area, which looks and feels more like a coffeehouse than a law office, to see Della, Neilmore or any of the thirty attorneys and paralegals who staff the Love is a House Foundation. They read poetry and talk over tea, coffee and Joan's famous red velvet cake. They wander through the law library, pound the keys of the research computers. They join in the childcare staff and read to the children or just let them play in the children's room or outdoor in the play park.

Love is a House is an enchanting two-story 25,000 square foot home that Marlon, Jamie, Neilmore, and Della brought from Terrence. Of course Jamie and Joan provided ingenious and tasteful guidance. The high-ceilinged workspaces and dining areas are airy, and the glass walls throughout pleasantly extend the House's elegant spaciousness. From the polished pine flooring to the skylights overhead, from the play park to the wooded hillside just beyond, the House feels connected.

Della and Jamie run the foundation as a self-help law center, fulltime, everyday.

"So even if the grants stop coming in, the House will be self-sustaining in less than three years. That is, of course, with the self-help law paralegal certification school fully attended," says Neilmore, summarizing the accounting report each of the women are looking at copies of.

"I'll say," Jamie cheers.

"Bravo," Marlon agrees. "There's never a shortage of folks who need public defenders, so the House will never be lacking there. I'll keep spreading the news throughout the county. How's private practice coming Neilmore, Della?"

"Terrific!" Neilmore lifts her wine glass. "Benton James is doing well."

"Really great! I've got the best Harvard grad Harlem ever sent as a partner!" Della raises her glass.

After the toast, she leaves the room to see a young woman who has been waiting patiently. No older than twenty years old, she's been clutching her little girl's hand for nearly an hour until her name is called. She is courteously greeted by a very tall, blonde woman.

"Good morning. How are you this morning? What a pretty girl. I will take you for a tour of Love is a House and then Della James will see you."

The young woman has never been here before but she had heard a lot about it. Everyone's talking about it and someone she used to ride the bus with told her at the grocery store this is where she needed to come. She works three jobs. The factory in the morning. The chocolate shop in the mall in the evenings. Housecleaning on Saturdays. She got evicted and moved in with her brother, only temporarily though. She has to make the best of her life on her own with her daughter.

The Love is a House Foundation is just the place for her.

As for Della, down the road in life she found true love. She was married and had a family.

The End

ABOUT THE *Author*

R. Lee Walker was born in Prentiss, Mississippi. He moved to Los Angeles with his mother and grandparents at an early age. He has a Degree in Economics from California State University at Dominguez Hills, and he has completed graduate work in business and education at the University of California at Los Angeles. Lee has produced hundreds of community talk shows and given to many charitable causes. He is also a world traveler.

AUTOGRAPHED BOOKS AVAILABLE THROUGH
R.LEE WALKER
P.O. BOX 47-0634
LOS ANGELES, CA90047

TOO GOD TO BE USED $24

Order Form

R. LEE WALKER
P.O. BOX 47-0634
LOS ANGELES, CA90047
(323)

Mail Check or Money Order to:

R. LEE WALKER

Name _____ Date _____

Address _____

City _____ State ____ Zip Code _____

Day Telephone _____

Evening Telephone _____

Book title _____

_____

Number of books ordered ____ Total cost _____ $ ____

Sales Taxes (CA add 8.25%) _____ $ ____

Shipping & Handling $3.00 per book _____ $ ____

Total Amount due _____ $ ____

Check   Money Order   Other Cards

Visa   Master Card   Expiration Date

Credit Card No. _____

Driver's Licence No. _____

_____   _____

Signature   Date

Allow 4 to 6 weeks for delivery.